W9-DDC-335

"You damn redhaired witch!" he growled. *"You'll belong to no one but me!"*

His mouth covered hers with the burning brutality of a brand, stamping his possession on the softness of her lips with the passion of a man driven too far. His lips left hers only to press hot, hungry kisses on her throat, cheeks and lids before returning to her mouth as if starved for the feel of it.

"God knows, I tried to send you away," he said raggedly, between the deliriously sensual kisses that made her feel as if she were slowly melting from the fire they built in her veins. His arms went around her, lifting and straining her flimsily clad body to his warmth while his lips continued their ruthless pillaging. "I knew damn well that if I kept you around I wouldn't be able to stop myself from taking you. Why the hell didn't you leave when you had the chance?"

Her hands slid slowly around his neck. "Kiss me, Jake. Please!"

WHAT ARE *LOVESWEPT* ROMANCES?

They are stories of true romance and touching emotion. We believe those two very important ingredients are constants in our highly sensual and very believable stories in the *LOVESWEPT* line. Our goal is to give you, the reader, stories of consistently high quality that may sometimes make you laugh, sometimes make you cry, but are always fresh and creative and contain many delightful surprises within their pages.

Most romance fans read an enormous number of books. Those they truly love, they keep. Others may be traded with friends and soon forgotten. We hope that each *LOVESWEPT* romance will be a treasure—a "keeper." We will always try to publish

LOVE STORIES YOU'LL NEVER FORGET
BY AUTHORS YOU'LL ALWAYS REMEMBER

The Editors

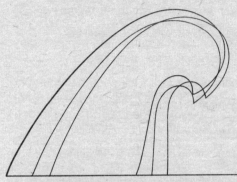

LOVESWEPT · 17

Iris Johansen

Tempest at Sea

BANTAM BOOKS
NEW YORK · TORONTO · LONDON · SYDNEY · AUCKLAND

TEMPEST AT SEA

A Bantam Book / September 1983

LOVESWEPT® and the wave device are registered
trademarks of Bantam Books, a division of
Bantam Doubleday Dell Publishing Group, Inc.
Registered in U.S. Patent
and Trademark Office and elsewhere.

All rights reserved.
Copyright © 1983 by Iris Johansen.
Cover art copyright © 1983 by Karen Assel.
*No part of this book may be reproduced or
transmitted
in any form or by any means, electronic or
mechanical,
including photocopying, recording, or by any
information
storage and retrieval system, without permission in
writing
from the publisher.*
For information address: Bantam Books.

ISBN 0-553-21617-1

*Published simultaneously in the United States and
Canada*

---

*Bantam Books are published by Bantam Books, a
division of Bantam Doubleday Dell Publishing
Group, Inc. Its trademark, consisting of the words
"Bantam Books" and the portrayal of a rooster, is
Registered in U.S. Patent and Trademark Office and
in other countries. Marca Registrada. Bantam
Books, 666 Fifth Avenue, New York, New York 10103.*

PRINTED IN THE UNITED STATES OF AMERICA

OPM   11   10   9   8   7   6   5   4   3   2

One

It was shortly before midnight when the yellow Volkswagen drew to a surreptitious halt on the deserted dock. A sudden gust of wind swirled the light fog in gossamer wisps around the small car, and caused the three artificial daisies fastened to the antenna to bob with jaunty cheerfulness. The headlights flicked out and the two women occupants peered cautiously out the windshield at the dimly lit pier that was their destination.

"I told you it would be all right," Jane Smith said cheerfully, grinning at the older girl, in the driver's seat. "Les said there wouldn't be anyone around at this time of night. There's only one night watchman, and he doesn't make his rounds for another two hours."

Penny Lassiter shook her head in exasperation, "Good Lord, Jane, this is a private marina. We could be arrested for trespassing. As for what else you're planning, they'd probably lock you up and throw away the key." She ran her fingers worriedly through her glossy brown hair, as she made one last attempt to dissuade her friend from the reckless course she had chosen.

"Nonsense," Jane said sturdily. "It may be technically illegal, but it's not as if I'm going to do anything really criminal. I'm doing this only to make a statement and gain enough publicity so that our petition will gain momentum. Besides, Les says that if I'm caught, the court will probably let me off with just a warning. They're always lenient with student demonstrators."

Penny Lassiter arched her eyebrow skeptically. "If it's so safe, why doesn't Les Billings do the job himself instead of letting you take all the risks?"

Jane smothered a little sigh as she gazed at her friend's worried face. She knew Penny had neither liked nor trusted Les Billings since he had joined their antinuclear society a few months before. Penny had a deep and sincere belief in what they were doing in trying to stop the building of the new nuclear power plant north of Miami, but Les Billings's ideas for accomplishing this aim were too radical and dangerous, in her estimation.

"Les couldn't be the one to do it," Jane explained patiently. "He was the one who went on board with the food delivery to case the ship. If anyone saw him, they might recognize him. It's much less likely that I'd be noticed."

"Case the ship?" Penny echoed incredulously. "My Lord, you even *sound* like an experienced second-story man." She bit her lip worriedly, her eyes on Jane's determined face. "Oh, damn, why did I have to let you become involved with this group at all? I should have known that you wouldn't be satisfied with marching or collecting signatures on a petition. You don't even know the meaning of halfway measures. You just rush in full speed ahead and think you can set the whole world right." She frowned. "Well, this is a little more serious than the collection of strays and derelicts you're always bringing home to the dorm. This could be big trouble."

"Yes, little mother," Jane said soothingly, "but it won't be, I promise you." She'd become used to Penny's maternal lectures in the year that they'd been roommates at the University of Miami, but she never made the mistake of becoming impatient or undervaluing the affection that provoked them. After losing her parents as a small child and living the gypsy life of an army brat under her grandfather's stern guardianship, she'd learned the hard way that love was a treasure that must never be taken for granted.

But Penny was steadily ignoring Jane's attempts to reassure her in this case. Her gaze was now traveling unhappily over Jane's petite figure, garbed in a black turtleneck sweater and dark jeans. Her small feet were encased in black canvas sneakers. In the black shapeless sweater, she looked nearer fifteen than twenty. "And you're insane if you think you won't be noticed and remembered if you're spotted on that yacht."

"Oh, but I've got that covered," Jane said mischievously, as she began tucking her short mass of curls beneath a black ribbed stocking cap. "Or I will have soon."

"I wasn't referring to your hair, damn it," Penny said in a thoroughly exasperated tone. She shrugged helplessly at Jane's disbelieving expression. It was a long-standing argument between them that Jane persisted in believing herself plain and insignificant, despite Penny's insistence to the contrary. Jane passionately hated the blazing red of her mop of silky hair that refused to do anything but curl riotously around her heart-shaped face, and she contemptuously referred to her strange golden eyes, framed in extravagant dark lashes, as "cat eyes." It was true that Jane's features, except for the huge eyes, were nondescript, but there was a certain tender curve to her lower lip and a mobile vitality to her expression that made them hauntingly memorable. In this case, dangerously so.

She reluctantly relinquished that argument, but immediately attacked from another angle. "You even look like some kind of a cat burglar. Is all this necessary?"

Jane grinned as she admitted sheepishly, "I don't

really know, but they always dress like this in the movies. I figured that there must be some reason for it."

"The whole affair makes no sense at all," Penny argued desperately. "Why pick on Jake Dominic's yacht for your demonstration? He has nothing to do with the building of the nuclear plant."

"Publicity," Jane said tersely. "Jake Dominic's just finished directing a motion picture that has a pronuclear slant. Les chose Dominic because he says that it will attract more attention than if we'd picked an ordinary businessman."

It was a fact that couldn't be disputed, much as Penny would have liked to discredit Billings in any way she could. Jake Dominic was the original golden boy. He had fallen heir to the fabulous Dominic shipping fortune at twenty-five and had promptly delegated authority in the corporation to continue to pursue his passion for directing films. In the past twelve years, Dominic's brilliance and fantastic success in his chosen field had been rivaled only by his scandalous and dissolute personal life. His wild escapades and numerous affairs had made him the sought-after prey of eager journalists in every country in the world.

"Yes, the newspapers will probably plaster the story all over the front page," Penny concurred gloomily. "Together with the account of your arrest and jail sentence."

Jane shook her friend's arm reprovingly. "Stop talking like that," she ordered cheerfully, "I'm not about to get caught. We have it all worked out." She reached in the back seat for her backpack, and as she strapped it on she continued soothingly, "Look, Penny, it will all be over in another hour. All I have to do is to row out to Dominic's yacht and climb the anchor line to get on board. I make my way to Dominic's cabin and write my message on the wall. Then I leave my backpack with the bomb in it in the cabin and row back to the pier." She tightened the strap of her backpack and smiled winningly. "Then you pick me up here and take me out for a well-deserved pizza. Your treat. It's another three days before I get my monthly insurance check."

Penny Lassiter flinched. "I wish you'd forget about that bomb, and just write your blasted statement on the wall," she said unhappily.

Jane shook her head stubbornly. "They might ignore the graffiti. We need to make them angry enough to make a fuss." She shrugged. "After all, it's not as if it were a real explosive. It's just a stink bomb. Les made it himself at the chemistry lab," she continued with satisfaction. "He says that when it goes off, it will cause a positively nauseating odor that will permeate the whole cabin and all the furnishings."

"Well, that should upset them enough to content even Les Billings," Penny said sardonically. "And what, may I ask, is Jake Dominic supposed to be doing while you're redecorating his cabin? No one could sleep through all that."

"No problem," Jane said blithely. "He's still in New York. There was a picture in the morning paper of Dominic and his latest mistress at Club 54." She frowned. "It's really too bad that he's not here. We'd get much more press coverage if he were on the spot."

"And it would also be much more dangerous," Penny said firmly, seeing the speculative gleam in Jane's golden eyes.

"Perhaps you're right," Jane said impishly. "If Dominic were here, I'd have to worry about stumbling over not only him but his latest bedmate. You know that Dominic always takes a woman on his cruises."

"You've been reading the gossip columns again," Penny said absently, her worried eyes on Jane's glowing face. "Jane, don't do this," she urged seriously. "It's not worth the risk."

"Of course it is," Jane said firmly, her golden eyes alight yet serene. "If you believe in something and it has value for you, then any risk is worthwhile." She leaned over and kissed Penny lightly on the cheek. "Relax, Penny. It's going to go off smooth as silk."

Penny shook her head slowly, her brown eyes oddly sad. "They'll probably crucify you," she said quietly. "This cynical old world doesn't have a place for people who care as much as you do, Jane."

"Then, I'll just have to *make* a place for myself, won't I?" she asked tranquilly, as she opened the door and jumped out. "Remember, be back here in one hour," she said, and she slammed the door. With a jaunty wave of her hand, she hurried toward the pier, where the rowboat waited.

Jane Smith cautiously opened the cabin door and slipped noiselessly inside, closing it after her with the utmost care. She leaned against the door in the stygian darkness for a brief moment and tried to still the rapid beating of her heart.

Despite her brave words to Penny, she was finding her first attempt at housebreaking—or was it yacht-breaking—a terrifying experience. She closed her eyes for a second and relived the panicky, helpless feeling she'd known as she had clung like a koala bear to the anchor line while she'd worked her way up hand over hand, inching toward the deck that had seemed a mile above her, while the threatening darkness of the sea waited for her first mistake.

Once she had reached the deck there was no difficulty in finding Dominic's cabin, thanks to the rough map Les had drawn, which she'd faithfully memorized. Still, it was a bit nerve-racking to be cast in the role of an intruder, even if your cause was just. Well, the sooner she got the job done, the sooner she could get out of here. Her eyes had now become used to the darkness, and she could dimly distinguish the shape of a king-sized bed a yard or so away and various pieces of furniture scattered around the room. On the far side of the cabin, she could discern the outlines of a large porthole. She would have to use the wall opposite the bed, she decided.

Undoing the straps of the backpack, she pulled it off and unfastened the pouch, extracting the can of red spray paint. She silently glided forward, going around the bed. The floor was obviously lavishly carpeted, she noted, as her sneakered feet sunk into the cushioned softness without making a sound. Her hands swiftly explored the paneled smoothness for art plaques or paintings. All she needed to do was to destroy one of Dominic's masterpieces, she thought grimly. She'd read that he was as ardent a collector of art as he was of women. The area was clear. She breathed a sigh of relief and backed away, aiming the nozzle of the spray can carefully. She fleetingly considered flipping on the light, but discarded the idea immediately. It would be too risky, and the message just had to be readable, not a thing of beauty.

She pressed her finger on the button and released a stream of paint, her arm moving in sweeping movements over the surface of the wall. It went quite quickly, and in a few minutes she neatly recapped the paint can and dropped it into her pouch. Her hands fumbled momentarily in the bag until she found the timer switch connected to the square metal box. She flipped the switch and then dropped the backpack carelessly on the floor.

Jane moved cautiously toward the door, wishing she could see well enough to hurry. Les had said the timer would give her forty-five minutes to get off the ship and back to the pier, but she didn't like to push it. It had taken her almost fifteen minutes to climb that terrifying anchor line.

"What the hell!"

The exclamation erupted from the king-sized bed, and Jane froze in horror as her eyes flew in the direction of the sound. The voice had been rough and masculine, and she experienced a ghastly sinking sensation as she realized to whom it must belong. She turned to flee, but it was already too late. The shadowy figure launched himself from the center of the bed in a tackle that knocked her neatly from her feet and pinned her to the carpet.

Jane struggled frantically, her fists beating at the

wide shoulders, her body writhing and kicking beneath the heavy masculine weight that was holding her helpless.

Suddenly she froze with shock as her touch communicated a frightening fact to her startled brain. My God! The man was nude! Her fists relaxed, and her palms slid tentatively over the hair-roughened chest, then glided exploringly over and around his hips to gingerly touch his hard buttocks. She jerked her hands away as if they'd been burned. It was true!

"Damn!" the man swore harshly, as his hands moved over the revealing softness of her body beneath the masculine attire. He roughly tugged the woolen cap from her silken curls, which smelled faintly of vanilla. "Not another one! This must be some kind of record. Two persistent women in one night!" His hands moved exploringly down her throat to the delicate curve of her shoulders. "Why not?" he drawled. "I'm finding your rather bizarre approach quite tantalizing."

Incredibly, Jane felt his loins lift and then rub with sensual aggression against her own, and she made a sudden movement of protest. He rapped out roughly, "Lie still, damn it!" Then his mouth covered hers.

Jane inhaled sharply in breathless shock as the warm hard lips pressed demandingly on hers, expertly parting them to invade her with savage intimacy. It was a bizarrely exciting sensation to be held helpless under that virile male body while his lips and tongue toyed with her own with ruthless expertise. The swiftness of his physical attack had left her dazed and bewildered, and the passionate onslaught of this nude stranger was suddenly met with a primal reaction from her woman's body. An aching warmth flooded her loins, and the tips of her breasts hardened in response to the stimuli his body was feeding her. Her lips opened yearningly to allow him eager access in his delicious love play.

He gave a deep groan of satisfaction, and his hands closed slowly over her small high beasts.

The intimacy of the caress caused her to stiffen in surprise. Abruptly Jane came to her senses. What was she doing? she wondered wildly. She was deliberately inviting the man to rape her! She resumed her frantic struggles against him with renewed desperation. The man's nude body was hardening in arousal, her movements acting as a provocation rather than a deterrent, she realized helplessly.

His mouth left hers and buried itself in her throat. "Be quiet, woman," he said thickly, his tongue teasing the hollow of her throat. "Give me what I want right now. I'm not in the mood for games tonight."

"No!" Her protest was smothered by his lips once more, and her mind searched frantically for an escape route. He was much too strong for her struggles to be anything but a minor annoyance to him. Her mind arrived at no answer, but her body acted instinctively to protect itself.

Her strong white teeth fastened on his sensual lower lip, and she bit down viciously, holding on like a terrier until he jerked his head away with a roar of rage. His weight was suddenly lifted from her, and she quickly jumped to her feet.

Jane experienced a moment of disorientation as her eyes eagerly searched the darkness for the outline of the cabin door. There it was! She made a swift movement toward the portal, but she had waited too long. The cabin flared into brilliant light.

Two

There was no question that it was Jake Dominic who stood at the light switch by the door, Jane thought resignedly. She had no problem recognizing the face from the newspapers. The black frown on his face gave his features a distinctly Mephistophelian cast. High cheekbones, sensual mouth, and dark expressive eyes lent him a satanic charm that was augmented by the black brows, one of which was slightly crooked, giving him a look of perpetual mockery. It was entirely in keeping with the cynical set of Dominic's mouth and jaded weariness in the ebony eyes. His crisp dark hair, worn slightly long, was ruffled from their struggles, and made him appear wild and careless.

Tall, broad-shouldered, slim-hipped, his whipcord body possessed a virile magnetism that was blatantly attractive. Jane's eyes dropped in fascination to the springy dark hair on his bronze chest, which gradually narrowed to a thin line as it reached his flat stomach. Her gaze flew quickly back to his face as her own face flushed scarlet. Dominic stood there as arrogantly unconcerned as if he were fully dressed, but she did not have the same *sang-froid*. She'd never been alone with a naked man, and she felt desperately uncomfortable—though perhaps she had better begin worrying about Dominic's emotional rather than his physical reaction. The man looked absolutely furious, black eyes blazing, nostrils flaring. His lip was bleeding freely where she'd bitten him, the sensitive flesh already starting to swell.

Jake Dominic's stormy gaze had become riveted by the lettering on the wall, and he stared at it incredulously. Jane turned and surveyed her handiwork with dismay. In three-foot cursive letters was the spray-painted slogan NO NUKES, and below it, in even larger letters, NUKES STINK. It was fortunate that it had been dark when she'd used the paint, she thought absently. If she'd seen the loveliness of the rich walnut paneling, she could never have brought herself to desecrate it.

Dominic's gaze returned to Jane, noting the tousled red hair and wide, frightened golden eyes. His eyes lingered for a moment on the swollen pink lips before he leaned indolently against the wall and wiped his hand over his bleeding lip. Though his face was still angry, there was a trace of amusement in his voice as he drawled softly, "Well, I'll be damned. If I haven't caught myself a baby terrorist."

Jane lifted her chin indignantly. "I'm no such thing," she argued defensively; "I'm a protester, not a terrorist." She gestured to the wall. "There's nothing in that to fill anyone with terror."

"It's a question of semantics, is it?" he asked lazily. "Regardless of what you may call it, you will admit that it's blatantly illegal."

She nodded reluctantly. "I suppose it is, technically."

"Technically, hell," he said roundly. "Vandalism, destruction of property, breaking and entering." He touched his lip gingerly. "And assault."

"Assault," she gasped, the angry color pinking her cheeks. "I was defending myself. You were trying to rape me."

"Rape!" Dominic exploded, his eyes sparkling dangerously. "I don't have to rape women. You were more than willing, my little terrorist.' Your hands were all over me."

"Only because I couldn't believe that I had a totally nude, bare-assed pervert on top of me," she shouted, her golden eyes blazing. "Why the hell don't you wear pajamas?"

A look of astonishment wiped the anger from his face. "I haven't worn pajamas since I was ten." His black eyes gleamed strangely. "You'll forgive my insensitivity, I trust. It's not often that I have a baby burglar drop in on me without invitation."

Suddenly her anger was gone, and she drooped disconsolately. What difference did any of it make? She had been caught, and she was frighteningly aware that the consequences could be more serious than she had dreamed before Dominic had reeled off that staggering list of charges.

"If you're through amusing yourself at my expense, I'd appreciate it if you'd just call the police and get it over with," she said dejectedly.

"Oh, yes, the police," Dominic said idly. "I suppose we had better call someone in authority." He reached for the white telephone on the table by the door and punched a number rapidly. After a moment he spoke into the receiver, his eyes still fixed on Jane's pale, weary face. "Hello, Marc. I'm sorry to wake you, but I think you'd better come down to my cabin. It seems we have an intruder." He replaced the receiver gently and turned back to Jane. "Now, while we're waiting, why don't you make yourself useful and clean up this lip? It's beginning to sting damnably."

Jane's eyes darkened with concern as she responded instinctively to the appeal for help. The lip was looking uglier by the minute, she noticed guiltily. It must be very painful. She impetuously moved forward to stand before him, touching the lip tenderly with a finger. "I hurt you," she said huskily, her eyes swimming with tears. "Please forgive me."

Her tone was patently sincere, and even Jake Dominic's cynical appraisal could detect no false note in the heartfelt apology. He smiled curiously, his dark eyes flickering. "I have the glimmering of an idea that you're not a very good terrorist, redhead." He took her hand and pulled her gently toward a door on the far side of the room. "Come along and play Florence Nightingale." He opened the door to reveal a luxurious bathroom, decorated in various shades of blue.

Jane followed him docilely into the small compartment, and while he half sat, half leaned on the cobalt-blue vanity counter, she carefully bathed the lip in cold water. Dominic flinched once, and her eyes clouded in distress. She made a low sound deep in her throat. Her reaction seemed to fascinate him, and for the remainder of the cleaning procedure, he studied her face with curious, narrowed eyes. When she'd finished, he slipped off the counter and, taking the washcloth from her, threw it carelessly into the sink.

"I'm obliged," he drawled casually. "It feels much better now."

Jane smiled in relief. "I'm glad," she said simply. "Now will you do something for me?"

His crooked eyebrow arched quizzically. "What?" he asked warily.

"Put on some clothes!" she said, the annoying color rising in her cheeks again.

He chuckled. "Oh, yes, you do have a hang-up about that. I'd forgotten. Well, as I can't leave my prisoner alone, you'll have to come with me." He strolled lazily out of the bathroom and, going to a built-in paneled closet, he slid back the door and took out a pair of dark trousers and pulled them on easily. He shrugged into a cream sport shirt and thrust his feet into a pair of Gucci loafers.

He turned and raised an eyebrow at Jane. "Satisfied?"

She nodded shyly, not meeting his eyes.

"You should be," he said teasingly. "My ass is no longer bare, and I assure you that I haven't been interested in kinky perversions for a number of years. That was quite unfair."

Then, as the color once more flooded her face, his expression became serious. "Go over there and sit down," he ordered quietly, gesturing to an easy chair covered in charcoal velvet that was situated just a few feet from the graffiti-covered wall. "I have a few questions that I want answered."

"Shouldn't we wait for the police?" she asked despondently, sinking obediently into the chair.

"I think you owe me an explanation," he said. "After all, it's my wall you ruined."

Dismayed, Jane's eyes swiftly flew to the paneling. "Is it really ruined?" she asked. "Isn't there anything we can do to save it? It's such a lovely wood."

Jake Dominic gave an exasperated sigh. "No, you've done too good a job on it. The paneling will have to be replaced."

"Who was the other one?" Jane asked suddenly, her golden eyes wide and inquiring.

"I beg your pardon?" Dominic said blankly as he sat down on a corner of the bed, facing her.

"You said that I was the second persistent woman tonight. Who was the other one?"

"It would hardly be gallant of me to reveal names," Dominic said dryly. "Let's just say that when I arrived on the *Sea Breeze* this evening, I had an unpleasant surprise in the form of a lady whose ego was a good deal keener than her intelligence." His lips twisted cynically. "She evidently thought that seduction could fan the dead embers back to life."

Denise Patterson, the gorgeous blond talk-show hostess, Jane guessed shrewdly. Dominic had evidently grown bored with her and broken off their affair last night. For a moment she felt a fleeting sympathy for the woman who'd thought she could hold Jake Dominic after he had tired of her. According to the gossip columns, Dominic's affairs were becoming even more ephemeral of late, and seldom lasted more than two weeks. Looking into that cynical, restless face, she could well believe it. When a man had seen everything, done everything, and had only to reach out to receive anything he desired, it was no wonder that he had become jaded.

That mocking devil's face was now frowning impatiently. "I'm not here to satisfy your curiosity. I believe that I was about to ask you a few very pointed questions. What's your name, redhead?"

"Jane Smith," she answered absently, thinking how the unbuttoned shirt stretched over the virile chest made him look more sensually naked than when he was totally nude.

Dominic's mouth twisted. "Not very original."

Her eyes flew to his face. "No, it's true," she protested. "Why would I lie? You'd find out anyway."

He shrugged. "Now the important question. Why me?"

"Your new film," Jane said simply. "It's got a pro-nuclear slant."

Dominic shook his head in disgust. "For God's sake, it's a blasted suspense thriller," he said harshly. "It's not a message film."

Her eyes met his in crystalline honesty. "It was the publicity angle," she said quietly. "We figured an incident with you would hit the front page."

"It might at that." He grimaced. "And who, may I ask, are 'we'?"

Jane's eyes widened in alarm. "No one," she said quickly. "This is all my idea; no one else was involved."

"It will probably go easier on you if you tell the police who else was responsible," he suggested coolly.

Jane shook her head at once. "I couldn't do that," she insisted stubbornly. "There wasn't anyone else."

For some curious reason, her answer seemed to please him. He regarded her with an enigmatic smile. "You know that you're in a great deal of trouble?" he asked as he studied the quivering of her soft pink lips and the raw fear in her golden eyes.

"I know," she said huskily, biting her lip nervously. "But . . . but there wasn't anyone else."

The cabin door was flung open, and three large, intimidating men rushed into the cabin. Jane looked up, startled, as the trio came to a screeching halt just inside the cabin door while they bewilderedly absorbed the scene in the cabin. One uniformed man in his late fifties, with gray-streaked hair and a tough, weathered face, was obviously in command of the other two, younger men, who were dressed in jeans and crew-neck sweaters.

Jake Dominic looked up, his brows lifting in mock surprise. "Hello, Marc. You certainly took your time about it," he said to the older man, lazily rising to his feet.

"I roused a few of the men—I thought we might need help," Marc replied absently, his stunned eyes taking in the crude message on the wall and then wandering back to the fragile-looking girl in the gray armchair.

"I think we can handle her between us," Dominic said, his lips twitching. "Captain Marcus Benjamin, may I present Jane Smith, girl terrorist."

Jane threw him an annoyed glance. "I wish you wouldn't keep calling me that," she complained.

"Sorry, Jane," Dominic said urbanely, his hands buttoning his cream shirt. "I'm still having problems with those semantics."

Benjamin's mouth tightened in irritation as he turned to face the two younger men, who were grinning irrepressibly at their captain's discomfort. "You can go back to bed, men," he said briskly. "Tell Jim to stay on duty on deck in case we need the launch."

The smiles were immediately wiped from the faces of the seamen at Benjamin's whiplike tone. They sketched a respectful salute and exited hurriedly.

Banjamin turned back to Jake Dominic and Jane, his expression grim. Jane shivered at the stern, authoritative figure the large man presented in his dark-blue uniform. "Now, what is this all about?" Benjamin asked, frowning.

"I was trying to determine that, when you and your bully boys burst into the cabin," Dominic said lazily. "It seems that Miss Smith took umbrage at my latest directorial effort and decided to make her opinions known."

"Very expensive umbrage," Benjamin said gruffly. "You'll have to send to Sweden to replace that panel." His gray eyes narrowed as Jane gasped in alarm. "What do you want done with her? I have a launch standing by to take her ashore. You'll have to go with her if you intend to press charges."

"That's right, I will, won't I?" Dominic observed noncommittally, his eyes on Jane's face. "Are you ready to face the music, Jane?"

Jane moistened her lips nervously, but her chin was set determinedly as she said valiantly, "Yes, Mr. Dominic." She slowly got to her feet. "It probably won't be as bad as all that," she went on bravely. "I hear the police go easy on student protestors."

"Then you've been misinformed," Benjamin said bluntly. "They regard a crime exactly the same, no matter who commits it. You're in big trouble, young lady."

Jake Dominic frowned and said impatiently, "You're frightening the child, Marc."

Benjamin shrugged. "There's no use in her fooling herself, Jake. There's a good chance that she'll go to jail for this night's work."

Jane could feel the last remaining color drain from her face at the captain's grim words. The situation was taking on all the nuances of a nightmare, and she knew a dizzying sense of panic.

"Will you stop intimidating the girl?" Dominic said roughly, "She's just a kid."

"No, it's all right," Jane said quickly, drawing a deep breath to steady the quivering in her stomach. Her hand was shaking as she nervously loosened the collar of her dark sweater. "I knew there would be some risk involved."

"But not this much," Dominic guessed shrewdly.

"I would have done it anyway," she said simply.

"Then you're an idealistic young fool," he said harshly.

Jane's eyes dropped before the scorching fire in his. "Perhaps," she whispered huskily, "but I'd still do it."

"Well, have you made a decision?" Benjamin asked impatiently. "Are you going to press charges, or are you going to let the girl get off scot-free?"

Dominic's eyes gleamed mockingly. "It's quite a difficult decision," he drawled. "It would be a bit of a bother going in to press charges." Jane looked up, her face lighting up with hope. "On the other hand, I wouldn't be a responsible citizen if I encouraged crime in our youth, would I, Marc?"

Benjamin made a sound that was half snort, half cough, and entirely derisive.

Dominic ignored the rude expression, and strolled casually over to Jane. He lifted her chin so that he could look into her eyes. "I rather favor a compromise," he said easily. "I'll not report the incident if you'll agree to come along on the cruise and work to pay off the damage."

Jane knew such a surge of relief that her knees felt as if they would not hold her. "Oh yes, please," she said eagerly. "I'll do anything you say."

"Anything?" Dominic goaded gently. "You're dangerously impulsive, Jane Smith."

The color once again flooded her cheeks at the teasing note in the deep voice, but her eyes were steady. "I'll work very hard, Mr. Dominic," she said earnestly. "It's very generous of you to give me the chance."

"Oh, I can be very generous when it pleases me," he answered coolly.

"And just what duties is Miss Smith to perform to earn that generosity?" Benjamin interrupted caustically.

Jake Dominic's hand released Jane's chin, and he turned away. "You'll find something for her to do, Marc," he said. "I'll leave it up to you."

"Will she be with us for the entire cruise?" Benjamin probed. "You planned to be gone almost two months."

Dominic smiled. "Oh, yes, the entire cruise, I think," he said gently, his black eyes gleaming. "After all, it was a very expensive panel."

Benjamin's eyes narrowed as he detected the restless flickering in the depths of Jake's ebony eyes. "I'll remind you of what you just told me," he said warningly. "She's just a child."

Swift anger darkened Dominic's face. "For heaven's sake, Marc, I'm not bringing her along to warm my bed," he said harshly. "She'll work her way, just as I said."

"And that's all?" Benjamin asked skeptically.

A reluctant smile touched Jake Dominic's lips. "Damn you, Marc," he said in grudging admiration, "you never give up, do you?" He shrugged. "She amuses me," he said simply. "Tonight is the first time in three bloody weeks that I haven't been bored out of my mind."

"So you're going to keep her around as some kind of pet?" Benjamin asked bluntly.

"Not as a pet," Dominic drawled, his brows arching mockingly. "Perhaps as a court jester."

"Hadn't you better ask the young lady if she agrees to your terms?" Benjamin asked dryly. "Perhaps she would have some objection to donning a cap and bells."

"I think she might prefer it to prison stripes," Dominic suggested silkily. "But yes, why don't we ask her?" He turned and gazed down at Jane's bewildered face. "What about it, Jane? Part-time slavery, part-time court jester. Is it a deal?"

There was a nameless challenge in the dark face that struck an answering spark in Jane's own adventurous spirit. After all, what was the man asking of her? She couldn't believe that a man of his sophistication and brilliance would find her entertaining for very long, but she couldn't deny that Jake Dominic exerted a powerful attraction. It shouldn't be an onerous task to spend time in his quicksilver presence. Besides, what choice did she have?

"It's a deal," she said quietly.

"What about her parents?" Benjamin asked. "You can't just shanghai the girl. They'll have you up for kidnapping, not to mention possible charges of corrupting a minor." He gave Jane's diminutive figure a disparaging glance. "She can't be over eighteen."

Jane bristled indignantly. "I'll be twenty-one in six months. And both my parents are dead. I can do as I choose."

"Good!" Dominic said briskly, his mouth quirking. "By the way, do you play chess?"

Jane's face was puzzled as she answered, "Why, yes, I used to play often with my grandfather."

Jake Dominic shot a sly glance at Benjamin. "You see, Marc," he said flippantly, "it's kismet."

"So it would seem," Benjamin said sarcastically. "Well, if you're set on keeping her, I'd better find her a place to sleep."

"Yes, you do that, Marc," Dominic said lightly, "Run along with Marc, Jane."

Jane stood up and obediently moved toward the waiting captain.

"Just a moment," he said, bending to pick up her backpack from the floor. "You forgot this."

Jane turned and held out her hand as he moved toward her.

"It's heavier than it looks," he said, weighing it casually.

"Oh, that's just the bomb," she said absently. Then, as she perceived both men's stunned expressions, she giggled helplessly. "It's just a stink bomb," she assured them, her face alight with amusement. She glanced at her watch. "There must be something wrong with the timer," she commented. "It should have gone off ten minutes ago."

"Let's not take any chances, shall we?" Jake Dominic asked testily, carrying the backpack over to the large porthole. He opened the porthole with one hand and drew back his arm to toss the bomb into the sea. "I have to sleep in here tonight."

Jane grinned and turned to follow Benjamin from the room.

The explosion as the bomb hit the water was deafening, and a shock wave rocked the ship, causing Jane to stumble against Benjamin. The captain instinctively put out his arms to catch her, but she tore away from him to whirl and stare in horror at the fiery glare that still illuminated the darkness beyond the porthole.

"Oh, my God!" she breathed, her eyes wide with shock. "Oh, God, I didn't know." How could Les do such a thing, she thought incredulously? If the bomb had gone off while Jake Dominic lay sleeping, he would surely have been killed, and who knew how many more would have been hurt? The blast had been awesomely powerful. If anyone had been injured, then she, too, would have been responsible. She had brought the bomb aboard. She had even set the timer. "Please, believe me," she pleaded brokenly, tears running silently down her cheeks. "I would never have done this; I didn't know."

Jake Dominic had been thrown against the easy chair by the force of the blast. Now he slowly straightened and looked at her grimly. "Oh, I believe you," he said tersely, his face a shade paler than it had been before. "You wouldn't have perched on top of a live bomb for almost an hour and then forgotten it existed, if you knew what your friends were up to."

Jane drew a quivering breath of relief. "I don't suppose you'll let me work off my debt now," she said uncertainly. "I can understand if you want to turn me over to the police. It was a terrible thing to do."

"You're damn right it was terrible," he said harshly. "It was also stupid, irresponsible, and dangerous. You should have your head examined to have become mixed up with a bunch of idiots who would perpetrate something like this. You obviously need a keeper!"

Benjamin's voice sounded from behind Jane. "Shall I ready the launch?"

Dominic's eyes flared angrily. "Hell, no," he said. "Why should I let a group of crackpots do me out of my personal slave? She goes with us. Now, get her out of here before I change my mind." He turned away and gazed out the porthole, his back taut and angry. "We'd better get underway at once and not wait until tomorrow. Someone's bound to have seen that explosion, and we don't want to answer questions from the Coast Guard."

"Right," Benjamin said laconically. He opened the door and, taking Jane by the arm, pushed the dazed girl ahead of him into the hall. Before he shut the door he spoke dryly to Dominic's expressively furious back. "I'll have to agree with you, Jake. She's certainly not boring."

Jane was pleasantly surprised by the interior of the cabin she was shown to on one of the upper decks. Though small and compact and obviously meant for crew instead of guest occupancy, it contained a narrow single bed covered with a bold gold-and-cream plaid spread, and a built-in Danish-modern night table was beside it. The floor was covered with an attractive beige carpet. There was a small matching chest of drawers to the right of the door, and the walls were paneled in the same rich walnut as the master suite.

Benjamin gestured to the door at the foot of the bed. "Shower," he said briefly. He turned away saying, "You'd better get some sleep. Your work day aboard the *Sea Breeze* will start from tomorrow on at 6:00 A.M."

"Captain?"

He turned back, his gray eyes inquiring.

"Are we really going to leave right away?" Jane asked hesitantly.

Benjamin nodded. "You heard Dominic. I'm not accustomed to disregarding my employer's orders, Miss Smith."

"No, of course you're not," she said absently, her golden eyes clouded with worry. "It's just that if I don't let my roommate know that I'm safe, she'll be absolutely frantic. Would it be possible for you to get a message to her before we set sail?"

"It might be arranged," he replied expressionlessly. "If you'll write down the phone number, I'll see what I can do."

"Thank you. I'd be very grateful," she said, accepting the pen and paper he extracted from his jacket pocket. She wrote Penny's name and their dormitory phone number on the paper, and continued, "It's a phone in the hall at the dormitory. If Penny's not at home, give any of the girls the message."

"And what message is that?" Benjamin asked dryly.

"Just that I had to go out of town for a few months, and that I'll write her as soon as I have the opportunity."

"Very discreet," he observed laconically. "I'll see that she's told, Miss Smith. Good night." The cabin door closed quietly behind him.

Jane looked longingly at the bed before turning away resolutely and striding briskly to the tiny shower cubicle Benjamin had indicated. She felt positively grimy from the perspiration and dirt resulting from the evening's strenuous activities. She would not climb between the sheets of that pristine single bed until she, too, was fresh and clean. Besides, she thought grimly as she stripped off her clothes and stepped beneath the spray of hot water, if she was to be summoned to work in just a few hours, it was quite doubtful that the stern, crisp captain would tolerate being kept waiting while she showered.

The fountain of warm water was deliciously soothing as it poured over her stiff muscles, releasing the coiled tension, which she had not even been aware of. The evening had really tied her in knots—and no wonder, she thought ruefully. In all her life she'd never lived through such a wild, madcap sequence of events.

Not that her life had ever been tame, she acknowledged wryly. Her grandfather had sworn that she attracted trouble like honey attracted bees, and she couldn't deny the charge. She had never tried to cause her grandfather problems, but she knew from the moment she came to live with him that his precise, well-ordered existence had altered irreversibly. It was her impulsiveness that had caused most of the problems, she thought gloomily. No matter how many times her grandfather had told her to think twice before she plunged into action, she could not live with the maxim. Perhaps her grandfather's life would have been more serene if his work as a colonel in the Army Corps of Engineers hadn't taken them to the four corners of the earth. There certainly had been more scope for mischief in the more primitive parts of the world, where she'd spent a good many of her formative years.

It had been even more difficult for her grandfather to understand his volatile young charge because he himself was not a warm or affectionate man, nor the least bit impulsive. Jane shook her head in self-reproach at the familiar pang, remembering the hurt and bewilderment she'd felt as a child when her advances had been met with such chilling formality. All that was in the past now. When her grandfather had died of a stroke eighteen months ago, she'd sworn never to indulge in maudlin self-pity.

She turned off the shower, stepped out of the stall, and reached for the fluffy white bath towel on the rack over the commode. Her grandfather would have been horrified at her present dilemma, she thought ruefully, patting herself dry. But the situation wasn't all that bad, when she thought about it. She would no doubt have to work extremely hard in the next two months, but she was used to that after her years with her grandfather. She would just take one day at a time, and soon her sentence on the *Sea Breeze* would be over.

Jane tossed the towel aside and, picking up the clothes she'd discarded, hung them up neatly in the tiny built-in closet. She was glad the jeans and sweater were sturdy and easily cared for, as were the briefs and bra. There was no telling when she would be able to scrounge a change of clothes on board.

She flipped out the light and slipped between the sheets, shivering as the crisp, cool material touched her bare skin. She plumped the pillow vigorously and nestled her fiery head in its softness with a sigh of content. The last thing she was conscious of was the low throb of the engines as the yacht put out to sea.

Three

The next morning promptly at six Captain Benjamin showed Jane a stretch of deck that appeared to extend into infinity. He then handed her a bucket of water, soap, and a scrub brush, and said silkily, "I won't waste your time on needless instructions. I know how eager you must be to get started on your new duties. Just carry on until you're told to stop. You did say that you'd be willing to do anything, Miss Smith."

Jane made a face at his straight, uniformed back as he strolled briskly away.

Four hours later she wished her defiance had taken a more tangible form. Very tangible. Like a swift blow with a sledgehammer on that distinguished, gray-streaked head. Jane dipped her scrub brush into the bucket of dirty water, then leaned forward on her hands and knees to vigorously scrub the wooden deck. She felt as if she must have prayed herself around the entire circumference of the blasted ship by this time. She brushed a strand of hair away from her forehead for the hundredth time, leaving still another smudge on her face. Though the denim material of her jeans was quite tough, it didn't offer sufficient protection for her knees. She was dreaming longingly of a lovely pair of thick athletic knee pads when a deep voice spoke over her head.

"So you're our big bad terrorist?" it drawled teasingly.

Jane looked up to see two long legs clad in sparkling white polyester standing directly in front of her. She sat back on her heels to regard balefully the vigorous young male torso and handsome face connected to those legs. Her tormentor was in his early twenties, dressed in the pristine freshness of white slacks and the beige waist-length jacket of a steward. His crisp blond hair and tanned features added to the impression of wholesomeness. The original Mr. Clean, Jane thought sourly, brushing a curl away from her perspiring forehead.

He squatted before her and looked with such frank, good-humored curiosity into her face that she was forced to admit grudgingly that there had probably been no malice in the remark. The clear blue eyes and sunny smile reflected only a gentle camaraderie.

Jane rubbed the small of her back wearily. "Aren't you afraid of being contaminated?" she asked dryly. "You're the first crew member except Captain Benjamin who has spoken to me this morning."

"It's not the men's fault," he said defensively, "The old man has passed the word that there's to be no fraternization."

"Then why are you disobeying the orders?" she asked, "Aren't you afraid of the captain, too?"

"Yep." He grinned amiably. "But I figure that I'm safe for the next thirty minutes or so. I just took the captain his lunch." He offered a large brown hand. "I'm Simon Dominic. Did you really plant a bomb in Jake's cabin?"

"Jane Smith." She started to put her small hand in his; then, noticing the dirt and soap on it, she withdrew it hastily. "Sorry," she muttered with a grimace, "I'm not very presentable. Yes, I did plant a bomb in Mr. Dominic's suite, but it was purely accidental."

Simon Dominic whistled soundlessly, his blue eyes

twinkling. "How intriguing. I can't wait to hear how you managed to plant a bomb accidentally."

Jane shook her head, smiling reluctantly. "It's a long story."

"And one you're not about to confide," he guessed.

"Not at the moment," she agreed, grinning. "Dominic? Are you related to Jake Dominic?"

"Very distantly," he confessed wryly. "Cousin Jake is about four times removed in blood and about forty million dollars removed in substance. He doesn't object to a bit of nepotism in the company, fortunately. My father is a vice-president of Dominic Shipping, and I'll be allowed to climb the corporate ladder myself as soon as I've put in my training period." He frowned in puzzlement. "Why aren't you using the electric scrubber? I'd think it would be far easier on your knees."

Jane's eyes darkened ominously. "The *Sea Breeze* has an electric scrubber?" she asked carefully.

"Several." Simon Dominic nodded. "Would you like me to get one for you?"

Jane drew a deep breath, trying to control the anger that surged through her. Benjamin had given her the brush and bucket with no mention of the machine that could have made her task a hundred times easier. Damn him!

She was tempted to agree at once to Simon's suggestion. She doubted if Benjamin would push the matter once she'd switched tools. She opened her lips to ask Simon to bring the machine and then closed them again, her eyes thoughtful. According to Benjamin's reasoning, his action in making her work as difficult as possible was entirely justified. Benjamin's code required that she accept her punishment and earn her place as a member of the crew. Jane could understand and respect his philosophy. She had no doubt that her grandfather, given the same circumstances, would have reacted in the same way. It was going to be a long two months, and an aching back and sore knees might be a small price to pay to earn the captain's respect.

"No," she said slowly, "that won't be necessary."

Simon Dominic shrugged. "Whatever you say," he agreed, rising to his feet. "Tell me, are terrorists permitted lunch, or are you only allowed bread and water?"

Jane smiled as she dipped her brush in the water. "I assume that I'll be eating all my meals with the crew from now on," she answered dryly. "The captain made it quite clear that I'm to have no special privileges."

"In that case, I'll brave his wrath and ask him if I can show you where the mess is located."

"Thanks, I'd appreciate that," Jane said warmly. She was going to like Simon Dominic.

With a blithe salute, the immaculate figure turned and walked back toward the bridge.

True to his word, Simon Dominic returned in an hour, and after accompanying her to her cabin, where she washed hurriedly and ran a comb through her hair, he escorted her to the crew's mess.

The mess was actually a large common room with a number of tables of varying size and a cafeteria-style serving area. The room was obviously used as a recreation area as well, she noted. There was a yellow-and-black dart board fixed on one wall, and one large table with leaves that could be opened to convert it into a Ping-Pong table.

Jane followed Simon through the serving line, conscious of the lull in conversation as she followed him to a small table, unloaded her tray, and sat down opposite him.

"I feel like Lady Godiva," she whispered as she poured dressing on the crisp garden salad.

"We should be so lucky," Simon joked, his blue eyes dancing. "They'll get used to you. We're not used to females on board ship, and you must admit your manner of signing on was a bit unusual."

"I certainly wouldn't recommend it," Jane answered, smiling. She took a bite of her salad and shook her head in amazement. "This dressing is absolutely fantastic. I imagine Captain Benjamin has no problem keeping his crew if the food is always this terrific."

Simon lifted his brows wryly. "The chow isn't always this good," he admitted. "Jake Dominic brings his own chef on these cruises, and he takes over the meal preparations from Max, our regular cook."

"Simon, could I ask a favor of you?" Jane asked impulsively.

"Anything," he promised lightly, adding, with a grin on his pleasant bronze face, "as long as it's not planting one of your 'accidental' bombs."

"I don't have any clothes," Jane said earnestly. "Do you have any old shirts or sweaters that I might use until I can get my roommate to send me some of my own?"

He looked doubtfully at her tiny figure and then at his own large frame. "You'd be lost in any of my clothes," he told her, shaking his head. "But I'll ask some of the other men and see what we can come up with."

"Thank you, Simon." Jane smiled radiantly. "I could see myself in these same jeans and sweater for the next two months." She gestured distastefully at her soiled jeans and the black sweater, which was now much the worse for wear.

"Well, you'll need something cooler than that sweater where we're going."

"Really? Where are we going?" she asked casually. Then, her eyes dancing: "For that matter, where are we now? I'm afraid I've been too preoccupied to even wonder."

"We're in the Gulf of Mexico," Simon replied. "We'll be cruising along the eastern coast of Mexico to the Yucatan and then possibly around Central America to Venezuela."

"I've never been to Mexico," Jane said dreamily. She grimaced as she came abruptly back to earth. "I'll probably not even get off the ship if Benjamin has anything to say about it."

"Oh, I don't know," Simon said optimistically. "Evidently he's lifted his nonfraternization rule, or he wouldn't have let me take you to lunch. Perhaps the old man is softening."

"Perhaps," Jane echoed skeptically.

At sundown that day she was no longer skeptical. She was sure that Benjamin had a will of iron and a heart to match. Every muscle and bone in her body ached. Her knees in particular were affected; they were swollen and bruised to a point of agonizing sensitivity. The sun had caught her face, and her nose was red and tender.

Jane gritted her teeth as she leaned over once again to soap the wooden deck. Benjamin had told her to continue scrubbing until he told her to stop, and she'd be damned if she'd quit before that time, even if she had to work through the night. She flinched as she put pressure on the wooden back of the brush and it rubbed against a blister on the palm of her hand. At least it was cooler, now that the sun was going down, she thought tiredly, as a vagrant breeze ruffled her hair, darkened with perspiration to nearly auburn.

For the past two hours she'd been in a haze of exhaustion and pain. Only sheer stubbornness had prevented the tears from flowing. She would rather fall flat on her face than admit defeat to that heartless monster of a captain.

A large shadow fell across the wet deck, but Jane didn't look up until Marcus Benjamin spoke.

"What the hell do you think you're doing?" he growled impatiently. "Do you realize that it's almost eight o'clock?"

She clenched her teeth and continued to move her brush, albeit a trifle slower. "I'm following orders, *sir*," she replied caustically. "I'm scrubbing the bloody deck, *sir*," She dipped the brush in the bucket and then brought it down hard on the deck, noting with satisfaction that a drop or two of the dirty water splashed on Benjamin's highly polished shoes. "If you'll kindly move, I'll finish my work, *sir*."

"Damn it, what do you think this is, a slave labor camp? You'll work a regular eight-hour day just like the rest of the crew," he said grimly.

Jane threw her brush in the bucket. "I thought I was the exception, sir," she said, meeting his eyes defiantly. "I believe I was told to continue my work until I was told to stop, Captain."

"I have other duties besides acting as a warden to you, Miss Smith," he said shortly. "I assumed you'd have the intelligence to stop at the end of a normal work day."

"Are you saying that I may stop for the day?" she demanded. "I want it quite clear, sir."

"Yes, you may stop working," he said between his teeth.

She struggled to her feet, staggering as her knees abruptly gave way. Benjamin instinctively reached out to help her, but she angrily shrugged his hand away. "I'm quite all right," she said lifting her chin proudly. She bent and picked up her bucket and brushed past him disdainfully, her back ramrod straight, and stalked away, leaving Benjamin to stare after her indomitable figure.

After luxuriating beneath first a hot and then a cold shower, Jane felt almost human. Using some of the emerald-green shampoo she found in the holder by the shower nozzle, she washed her hair until it was squeaky clean. Wrapping the towel around her torso and another around her hair, she left the cubicle and crossed to the bed. She settled cross-legged on the bed and examined her knees. They were definitely swollen, and faintly purple. By tomorrow it would be like kneeling on knives to rest her weight on them, she thought gloomily. Why hadn't she unbent and asked Benjamin to change her duty? She instinctively shook her head at the thought. No, she wouldn't give him the satisfaction of seeing her beg, no matter what the consequence.

A brisk knock sounded at the door, and she called

out, "Just a minute." She grabbed the improvised toga she'd fashioned from a bed sheet. Ripping off the towel and slipping on the toga, she padded bare-foot to the door.

Simon Dominic stood on the other side, his arms piled high with various articles of clothing. He grinned as he beheld her toga-clad figure and turbaned head. "That's very exotic. I doubt if anything the boys contributed will be as alluring."

"Oh, Simon, thank you," she said gratefully, reaching for the clothes. "Won't you come in?"

He shook his head. "Your cabin is officially out of bounds, per Captain Benjamin," he said. "I just brought these by. I hope some of them will do."

"They'll have to," Jane answered lightly. "Thank everyone who donated to the cause, will you?"

Simon nodded, his blue eyes sympathetic. "I'm afraid that I've got bad news for you." He spoke hesitantly. "Captain Benjamin told me to give you a message when he knew that I was coming down here. You're to report to the lounge in thirty minutes for your secondary duties."

For a moment Jane didn't realize what he meant. Then she understood. Secondary duties. Jake Dominic must have sent for her to play court jester. Well, he was not going to find her very amusing tonight, she thought tiredly. She would probably be back in her cabin in an hour.

Simon's face was grim. "There's absolutely no call for this," he said indignantly.

"These duties will be very light," she assured him soothingly. "Thank you for caring, but it will be all right. Honestly. I'll see you at breakfast tomorrow, Simon."

"Right," Simon said, turning away with a comradely wave of his hand.

When Jane appeared in the lounge some forty-five minutes later, she felt that she fully resembled the buffoon of Jake Dominic's original simile. Her khaki pants were rolled up in thick, bulky cuffs, but there was nothing she could do about the baggy seat or the looseness of the waist. The thin cream sweater that she had teamed with it came almost to her knees, and the long sleeves kept slipping down from her elbows, where she had pushed them. Her hair was still slightly damp, and curled in wild ringlets all over her head. Jane had smiled philosophically when she'd caught sight of herself in the mirror in the cabin. There was no way she could compete with the gorgeous and well-dressed women of Jake Dominic's acquaintance even when she was at her very best. What difference did it make if she looked like something out of a circus?

Jake Dominic was sprawled in an enormous brown leather easy chair, his feet propped on the matching hassock. She noted with some disgruntlement that he looked devastatingly attractive in dark fitted pants and a red crew-neck sweater.

He looked up absently from the script he'd been studying, as she came in the door. His dark eyes widened, and his lips twitched uncontrollably as he leisurely looked her over from her water-stained canvas tennis shoes to the unruly red curls. He tossed the script aside and said mockingly, "I must admit you present an amusing spectacle, but you really shouldn't have gone to all this trouble."

Jane strode forward to stand directly in front of him, her hands planted belligerently on her hips. "Mr. Dominic, I'm very tired. I haven't had any dinner yet, and I have a wretched sunburn that's not improving my disposition. You know very well that I have nothing to wear, and I would appreciate your not making cheap jokes at my expense."

He arched an eyebrow quizzically. Then his eyes narrowed and the laughter was abruptly banished from his face. "I'm a bit tired myself, redhead," he answered softly. "I've been working on this awful script all day trying to draft some cohesion into the greatest hodgepodge of symbolistic tripe it's ever been my misfortune to read. I'm not sunburned for the simple reason that I've not stuck my head out of this room all day. I will grant, however, that I do have one advantage over you other than my sartorial elegance. I have eaten dinner."

He rose with swift grace and, taking her by the wrist, pulled her behind him as he strode with long steps to a beautifully carved mahogany bar. Pushing her firmly onto a cushioned stool covered in antique-gold velvet, he went behind the bar and said briskly, "We can remedy that if you'll settle for sandwiches and coffee. Will ham do?"

She nodded dazedly. "That . . . that will be fine," she stammered, as she watched him kneel before the copper-toned portable refrigerator under the bar and withdraw an oblong plastic container that opened to reveal pink ham sliced paper-thin. He brought another container from a side cabinet that contained deliciously crisp hard rolls. He built her a sandwich with quick practiced movements, adding tomato, lettuce, and mayonnaise at her request. He poured her a cup of coffee from a thermos jug at the end of the bar and set the lot before her with a little flourish.

"Anything else?" he asked blandly. "I believe there's some caviar and pâté de foie gras in the refrigerator."

"No, thank you," Jane said, making a face. "That sounds perfectly dreadful. I've never understood how anyone could really enjoy caviar."

"Neither have I," he confessed, his dark eyes twinkling. "But my chef is an incurable snob and insists that no self-respecting multimillionaire should have a refrigerator unstocked with caviar."

Dominic poured himself a cup of coffee, and, leaning his elbows on the bar, watched her wolf down the sandwich with every evidence of enjoyment. "You *were* hungry," he commented. "What caused you to miss dinner?"

Jane looked up to meet his eyes before she replied noncommittally, "I was busy." She was not about to complain to Mr. Dominic about her treatment at his captain's hands.

He touched the tip of her sunburnt nose with a light finger. "I see Marc's found you something to do outside," he said casually. "That should be a welcome change after burrowing in college classrooms all winter."

Jane's mouth curved in a wry smile. It was obvious from his remark that Jake Dominic was ignorant of the precise nature of the duties Captain Benjamin had assigned her. Well, why should he be apprised of such pedestrian arrangements? It was the duty of the captain and the crew to see that everything ran with clockwork efficiency on the *Sea Breeze* so that its owner would not suffer a moment of discomfort or displeasure.

"Yes, it's quite a change," she agreed dryly. She took a sip of the excellent coffee. "Why are you working? I thought you were supposed to be on vacation."

"I want to get these script changes out of the way and get it back to the producer," he said, lifting his cup to his lips. "It should only take a few days, and then I'll be free to relax."

Jane looked thoughtfully into the restless dark eyes. Did he ever really relax? she wondered idly. She'd seen no evidence of it in the brief time she had been acquainted with him. He seemed charged with a leashed vitality and a crackling virility that should have been disconcerting to a girl of her limited experience of men. Oddly enough, this was not the case. Perhaps it was the unconventional nature of their first meeting that had dispensed with the usual reservations that would have beset a relationship between two such opposites. At any rate, she felt as completely at ease with this man as if she'd known him from the cradle.

"If you're so busy, I'm surprised you bothered to send for me," she remarked as she finished the last bite of the sandwich and pushed the plate aside.

"All work makes Jake a dull boy," he misquoted audaciously, his black eyes gleaming. "After working all day on that mishmash of a script, I felt the need for the soothing pursuit of pure logic. In short, Jane Smith, you're going to give me a game of chess."

She grimaced ruefully. "If you're looking for a game

involving logic, you've made an unfortunate choice for a partner. My grandfather used to nearly tear his hair out in frustration at my game."

"All the better," Jake Dominic said promptly, with a tigerish grin. "It will be a little like destroying that damn screen writer in effigy."

"What a charming idea," she said with sweet irony. "With my being said effigy, I assume?" A glint of determination shone in the golden eyes as she cradled her cup in her hands and looked him directly in the eyes. "It may not be as easy for you as you believe. I don't give up easily, Mr. Dominic."

"I'd be disappointed if you did. I don't enjoy victory if it's handed to me on a plate." He finished his coffee with one swallow and put his cup on the bar. "Shall we get to it?" he asked politely, gesturing to a game table in the corner.

"Why not?" Jane felt a thrill of anticipation run through her that was far in excess of the challenge involved. What was it about the man that made a simple game take on such excitement and significance?

Setting her empty cup on the bar beside his, Jane slipped off the stool and followed him to the game table, her eyes flitting curiously around the large lounge.

It was a singularly beautiful room. Its focal point was the magnificent Persian carpet that covered the highly polished wooden floors. The conversation center consisted of a long couch crafted in rich, tufted brown leather, and two huge easy chairs with their own matching ottomans. The walls were paneled in the same gorgeous walnut Jane had noted in the other cabins. On the walls were several paintings that were obviously originals.

Jane paused in front of one particularly fine El Greco, admiring, as she always did, the astonishing excitement he could convey in a simple landscape.

Jake Dominic retraced his steps to stand beside her, his eyes on her absorbed face. "You like El Greco?" he asked, his crooked eyebrow arching mockingly. "I should have guessed. He, too, was something of a revolutionary."

Jane ignored the gibe as she continued to gaze enthralled at the painting. "He cared so passionately," she said slowly. "You can see it in every brushstroke. Thank God you didn't have this in your cabin. I had nightmares about spraying one of your masterpieces by accident," she confessed with a shudder.

"If you had, I would have broken your reckless little neck," he told her with grim sincerity.

"I tried to be careful," she said defensively. "I examined the entire area before I sprayed."

"It was so dark you couldn't see a thing," he said tersely. "How could you be sure?"

"The same way I knew you were naked," she said unthinkingly. "I ran my hands over it."

Then, as she realized what she had said, scarlet flooded her face. She avoided the spark of amusement in Dominic's dark eyes and rushed on desperately. "I'm ready to play now."

His lips twitched as he said solemnly, "It's a pity you weren't ready to play then. If you'll recall, I was more than willing."

Jane lifted her chin, swept with regal dignity to the game table, and seated herself sedately. "You know what I mean," she said severely.

He nodded as he seated himself opposite her. "I hope your game is more concise than your words, Jane," he drawled. He opened a drawer in the table and drew out a carved teak box. "You could be in deep trouble in no time at all."

The next few hours proved this comment to be depressingly true. It took a relatively short time for Jane to determine that she was hopelessly outclassed by Jake Dominic. Her grandfather had been a good, solid methodical player, but this man was clearly in the master class. His strategy was as complex and ruthless as the man himself. She knew herself to be a fairly good player, with flashes of almost intuitive brilliance. Her fatal weakness lay in that streak of impulsiveness that had been the bane of her grandfather's existence. Even so, at the end of two hours of play, when Jake Dominic had inevitably put her in check, she felt that she'd given a reasonably good account of herself.

Jake leaned back in his chair, one long, graceful hand toying idly with her queen. "You know that you could be much better than you are?" he asked quietly. "All you need is a little self-discipline."

"I know," she agreed, making a face. "It was drummed into me often enough by my grandfather. But I can't bring myself to play that way. It would take all the fun out of it."

"Even if it would eventually furnish you with the fruits of victory?" His eyes were curiously searching.

"I'm not that goal-oriented," she said casually. "I'd much rather enjoy myself along the way."

"I'm afraid I can't agree with your philosophy." His mouth curved in that familiar mocking smile. "I always find winning worthwhile. I make a habit of it."

She already knew that. Jake Dominic had devoted the same single-minded effort to his chess game that he would to any more serious project.

Jane smiled happily as she helped him to collect the ivory chess pieces and replace them in their velvet-lined box. "Well, the contrast of viewpoints makes for an interesting game," she commented, and concentrated on putting each piece properly in its indented place in the box.

Dominic's eyes flickered with amusement as they fixed on the girl's almost childishly intent face, her pink tongue unconsciously protruding from the corner of her mouth as she gravely put the last piece in the box and closed the lid carefully.

"Yes, it makes for an interesting game," he repeated slowly, accepting the box from her and replacing it in the drawer.

Jane smothered a yawn as she pushed back her chair and stood up. Now that the tension of the game had ended she was suddenly overpoweringly sleepy. "Thank you for the game, Mr. Dominic," she said, sounding like a polite little girl. "If you don't mind, I'll say good night now."

"Would you like some more coffee?" he offered lazily, rising to his feet. He looked at his watch. "It's only a little after eleven."

She shook her head firmly. "I must get to bed," she said with a grimace. "I have to get up at six."

"Oh, yes, I'd forgotten," he replied absently, with a trace of annoyance in his voice. "Run along to bed, then," he said curtly. "But be sure you report here at eight sharp tomorrow evening."

"Tomorrow?" she asked, smothering another yawn. "You want me to come again tomorrow evening?"

"I said so, didn't I?" he asked testily, his expression half amused, half annoyed at her obvious lack of appreciation of his desire for her company.

"Okay," she muttered inelegantly, turning to leave.

"Jane!"

She half turned, to gaze at him like a sleepy kitten from those great golden eyes.

"See that you eat dinner tomorrow. I refuse to wait on any woman two nights in a row."

Four

That first day set the pattern for the ones that were
to follow. Jane's second day scrubbing decks was
even more uncomfortable than the first. The pain in
her bruised knees was agonizing, and seemed to
grow in intensity as the day wore on. The only relief
from the misery of pain and exhaustion came from
the increasingly open display of sympathy and support from the other members of the crew.

Simon had introduced her to a number of the
crew at breakfast that morning, and Jane had found
them to be a genial and friendly group, altogether
different from the rough, tough, blustery image that
she had always had of men who made their liveli-
hood on the sea. That they all possessed a streak of
gallantry she was to learn later in the day.

One by one, with seeming casualness, they wandered by the area where she was working. And always they brought gifts, ranging from a drink from
a thermos of coffee, to the presentation of a panama
hat to shade her from the sun and a pair of rubber
gloves to relieve her chapped and reddened hands.
Though the gifts were invaluable in themselves, it
was the sympathy behind them that gave her the
strength to complete that second agonizing day.

Her time with Jake Dominic in the evenings became a priceless oasis in the desert of those next few days. No matter how excruciatingly tired she was at the end of the day, she had only to open the door of the lounge and see Jake look up with that mocking smile to feel a rush of new vitality. It was inexpressibly soothing to sit over the chessboard and watch the wary flickering behind those ebony eyes as she presented him with an unexpected challenge, or to listen to his amusing stories of life on the set as they sat over coffee. Jake Dominic continued to treat her with the affectionate indulgence that he might show a precocious niece, and this arrangement met with her entire satisfaction. She was fully aware that in any other role, he would be a highly dangerous commodity. She doubted her ability to handle any encounter with the much-publicized rake of the tabloids. She much preferred the Jake Dominic who teased her about her cat eyes, trounced her soundly at chess, and let her leave him at the end of the evening with no more than a casual wave of his hand.

But by the fourth day not even the anticipation of the evening to come could dull the sheer agony Jane was experiencing. She'd borrowed two elastic bandages from Simon to bind her knees, which were now swollen twice their normal size and were a livid purple. The bandage provided a little protection, but as the day progressed she began to feel a trifle nauseous from the pain. She did not bother to go to lunch that day. She merely crawled to the rail and sat leaning against it, her eyes shut against the glaring noonday sun. She gently massaged her left kneecap, which for some reason appeared to be in worse condition than the other. She really must eat dinner, she thought wearily. She'd need all the strength she could muster to get through tomorrow.

But by evening it didn't seem to be worth the effort to make her way to the mess. After a quick shower, she rebandaged her knees and lay down on her bunk to nap for the two hours' respite before she had to report to the lounge. Luckily she took the precaution of setting the alarm on her clock, for when she collapsed on the bed she fell into an exhausted sleep.

The alarm woke her with its strident ring, and for a moment Jane was tempted to shut it off and roll over and go back to sleep. Then she sat up and began to dress in the oversized khaki trousers that she had worn that first evening. She grabbed her own black turtleneck sweater, which she'd washed out by hand the night before, and slipped it on. She went into the bathroom to run a comb through her hair, and her reflection in the mirror over the sink sent a shiver of distaste through her. She looked like a sick cat, she thought gloomily. She spent the next few minutes massaging her pale cheeks with the rough terry towel to restore the color to them.

When she opened the door to the lounge ten minutes later, she drew a deep breath and fixed a bright smile on her face before she strolled forward, making a conscious effort not to hobble.

Jake Dominic was sitting at the bar, a glass of bourbon in his hand and an impatient frown on his lean dark face. Tonight he was wearing faded jeans that hung low on his hips and hugged the muscular line of his thighs with loving detail. His navy cotton shirt was left carelessly unbuttoned almost to the waist, and Jane's eyes were drawn in fascination to the triangle of dark wiry hair on his powerfully muscled chest.

Jane had a fleeting memory of the rough virile feel of that hair against her fingertips. She felt a sudden warmth in her cheeks, and she looked away hurriedly.

"You're thirty minutes late," Jake said. "I was about to send someone to get you."

She made a mocking bow. "Forgive me, O honorable master," she said in a singsong, lowering her lashes demurely. "Your lowly servant humbly begs to be excused for this grievous misdemeanor."

A reluctant smile curved his lips. "Impudent scamp," he charged. "Be careful, redhead. One of these days I'm going to teach you a little respect." He rose to his feet and swallowed the rest of his drink.

"What do you call our chess games?" she asked lightly. "If you ever think of a more severe lesson than you dish out over that chess table, I may not show up at all."

A flicker of annoyance touched Jake's face. "You'll do as you're told," he said coolly. "I own you, remember?"

Perhaps it was her weariness that urged her to prick at that arrogance. "But only for two months," she reminded him sweetly. "Our agreement was just until the end of the cruise."

His face became even darker, and Jane wondered idly what had served to put him in such a savage humor. Surely the fact that she was a little late couldn't have annoyed him to this extent.

An unpleasant smile twisted his lips. "That's right, redhead," he said silkily. "It was just for the duration of the cruise. But I don't believe I specified the exact length of the cruise. Who knows—I may feel the need for an extended rest." His eyes flickered moodily. "How would you like to continue with your duties for the next six months?"

Jane gave him a distinctly skeptical look. "That would be a greater punishment for you than it would be for me," she said serenely. "I'd wager you'd be bored to tears in no time, Mr. Dominic. You're not exactly the playboy type."

"There are a number of people who would disagree with you," he said bitterly. "Don't you read the gossip columns?"

"I'm not saying that you don't try to maintain the pose," Jane said kindly. "But you're much too dynamic to be really successful at it."

Jake Dominic's dark eyes narrowed. "You're very confident of your own powers of judgment," he said softly. "I think you should be aware that I heartily dislike being considered predictable, little one." There was such a wealth of menace in his tone that Jane took an involuntary step backward.

The action brought a glint of satisfaction to his eyes. "If you're through with your amateurish psychoanalysis, I suggest we get on with the game," he said coldly, and he turned and walked away.

The game that night bore no resemblance to the ones that had preceded it. Jake Dominic was out for blood tonight. From the first move it was clear that he meant to vanquish her in the most brutal and humiliating method possible. In a little under an hour he had her in check.

Jane looked across the table into the ebony eyes gleaming in triumph, and said ruefully, "I guess you put me in my place. Remind me not to make you angry again. My self-esteem can't take it."

Some of the ruthlessness faded from his face, to be replaced by an odd watchfulness. He shook his head incredulously. "Don't you know that you're supposed to be ground beneath my heel?" he asked dryly. "What does it take to put you down, Jane?"

Jane shrugged, her smile shaky. "Oh, I'm suitably chastised, I assure you. You can be a very intimidating man, Mr. Dominic."

"Jake, damn it," he said impatiently. "What's the point in addressing me so formally, when you know I get nothing but cheek from you?"

"Jake," she repeated, the name sounding strangely intimate on her lips. She pushed back her chair and rose slowly, her knees stiff from inactivity. "Well, Jake, I believe I'll call it a night. I'm afraid your court jester isn't providing you with the proper degree of amusement this evening. Perhaps another time."

The dark eyes flared with annoyance. "It's early yet. Stay a bit," he ordered arrogantly. "I'll give you another chance."

She shook her head. "Not tonight," she said, turning away.

Jake's hand snaked out to grasp her wrist, obviously meaning only to stop her, but the stiffness of her legs caused her to be momentarily unbalanced, so that her left limb rammed into the table leg. A flash of hot agony shot through it, and a cry of pain broke from her.

Jake's eyes widened in surprise. "What the hell!" he exclaimed, his hand loosening around her wrist. His lightning glance took in the pasty color of Jane's face and the helpless quiver of her lips. "My God, what the hell happened?" he asked roughly. "You look like you're about to pass out."

She shook her head as the wave of nausea gradually subsided. "I hit my leg," she said shakily. "I'll be all right in a minute." She sank back into her chair and closed her eyes, breathing deeply to still the sudden quivering weakness in her stomach.

With a muttered oath Jake was out of his chair and kneeling in front of her, his hands swiftly rolling up the loose leg of her khaki trousers.

She opened her eyes in sudden alarm and reached down to stop him. "No," she said quickly. "I'll be fine. Just give me a moment."

Jake's dark eyes were grim. "You're not going to stop me, Jane, so don't try," he said harshly. "You barely touched that table leg and yet you're almost fainting with pain. I'm going to find out why."

His determined gaze held hers for a long moment before she dropped her eyes. She couldn't fight him right now, she thought wearily. She hadn't the strength.

He had rolled the cuff over her knee, and now his swift, dextrous hands were unrolling the elastic bandage. He unwrapped the last layer of cloth and pulled the bandage away to reveal the ugly purple swelling of her kneecap.

"Good God!" he swore harshly. "What the hell have you done to yourself? That knee must be terribly painful."

Jane wet her lips nervously with her tongue. "It's not that bad," she said. "It will be fine in a few days." She tried to cover the discolored bruise with her trouser leg, but he stopped her, an ominous frown clouding his face. His sharp glance had now noted the slight thickness beneath the other pant leg, and with a terse but descriptive obscenity he proceeded to roll it up. His face was rigidly controlled as he unwrapped the second bandage and saw the swollen knee.

He sat back on his heels, and his gaze traveled from knee to knee with incredulous eyes. "You've got to be the most stupid little bitch on the face of the earth!" he said explosively. "Haven't you got the sense to know that those bruises need attention? You shouldn't even be on your feet, for God's sake."

"They'll be all right," she insisted stubbornly. "I'll bathe them in cold water when I get back to my cabin." She started to rise, and he pushed her unceremoniously back into the chair.

"Stay where you are," he ordered. "I don't want you on your feet again until you have my permission. Which probably won't be for at least a week," he added grimly, as he eyed the abused knees sourly.

"That's not possible," Jane said stubbornly. "I've got to work tomorrow."

Jake's lips were taut with anger as he remarked sarcastically, "Your devotion to duty is praiseworthy, but I run things around here, if you recall. You'll do what I say and like it. I'll tell Marc I'm sending you to bed for the next week."

"No!" she cried forcefully, her golden eyes blazing. "I won't have Captain Benjamin think I came running to you because I couldn't take it. I'm going back to work tomorrow, and you can't stop me!"

Jake's eyes narrowed at her words. "What can't you take, Jane?" he asked with the softness of a stiletto sheathed in velvet. "Why should Marc think that you'd run to me?"

"I can take anything your precious captain hands out," Jane said, breathing raggedly, "anything! And neither you nor anyone else is going to keep me from being on that deck in the morning!"

"We'll see about that," he said. "But right now you're going to tell me what you're going to be doing on that deck tomorrow."

"Why, scrubbing it, of course," she said bitterly,

suddenly reckless. "Miles and miles of it. How else do you think my knees would get like this?"

Jake Dominic went suddenly still. "You're saying that Benjamin has had you scrubbing decks on your hands and knees for the past four days?"

Jane tossed her head. "Why not? Fresh sea air, sun, healthful exercise," she enumerated caustically. "As you said, quite a change from the classroom."

Anger flared in the dark eyes. "Damned if I don't almost see why Marc did it," he said between his teeth. He rose to his feet and crossed to the phone extension at the bar and dialed rapidly. He spoke into the receiver. "Marc, I want you in the lounge immediately." Without waiting for a reply he replaced the receiver and turned to look at her.

Jane looked infinitely vulnerable lying back in the chair, her cheeks pale, her diminutive body in its oversized garments slight and fragile. The only signs of strength were in the defiance in her eyes and the indomitable set to her soft pink mouth.

"Why didn't you tell me?" he asked curtly.

She lifted her chin. "It wasn't your concern. For that matter, it still isn't. It's entirely between Captain Benjamin and myself."

He gazed at her in incredulous anger. "Damn it," he said harshly. "I own the *Sea Breeze*. I employ every person aboard her, and you say it's not my concern when my captain abuses you?"

"I am not abused," she said crossly. "I wish you'd just stay out of it." She tightened her hands on the arms of the chair and attempted to lever herself into a standing position.

"Damn it, can't you ever obey orders?" he roared. He crossed the room in four strides and swung her up in his arms, ignoring her startled gasp.

She started to speak, but he cut off her words. "Shut up! Just shut up!" He carried her to the brown leather couch in the center of the room and dropped her on it with all the gentleness of one disposing of yesterday's garbage. "Now, stay there!"

Jane pulled herself into an upright position, very

affronted by this undignified treatment, and opened her mouth to tell him just what he could do with his orders. This extremely hazardous course of action was interrupted by the arrival of Marc Benjamin.

The captain looked his usual commanding, unruffled self in his dark-blue uniform. His keen gray eyes impersonally noted Jane's presence on the couch, before he turned his attention to Dominic. "You wanted to see me?" he asked composedly.

Jake crossed to the bar and poured himself a brandy. "You could say that," he said tersely. "I hear you've been acting like a virtual Captain Bligh with our reluctant guest, here."

"I didn't say that!" Jane protested hotly. "I told you this was none of your business." She turned to the captain and said quickly. "I'll be on deck tomorrow at the usual time, Captain Benjamin."

"You needn't try to protect me, Miss Smith," Benjamin said coolly. "I'm quite capable of making my own explanations."

"Protect you!" Jane sputtered furiously. "I'm not protecting you, my dear Simon Legree. I just want no interference in what is strictly a private battle. I have no intention of winning by default."

Benjamin didn't pretend to misunderstand her. "It seems you've done just that, whether you like it or not," he answered impassively.

"Not on your life," Jane said emphatically, her eyes burning like a flame in her white face.

"I can't believe this." Jake came forward to stand beside the couch. "If you'll stop squabbling like two kindergarten children, I'd like that explanation, Marc."

The captain shrugged. "There's nothing to make a fuss about, Jake," he said calmly. "Miss Smith and I were just having a little battle of wills. I'll change her to another duty tomorrow."

"You'll do no such thing!" Jane cried, struggling to get to her feet.

Jake pushed her back on the couch. "Be still!" he ordered roughly. He turned to Benjamin and asked grimly, "What type of work did you imagine she could do with legs like these?" He reached down and pulled the khaki pants up to reveal her swollen kneecaps.

Benjamin gazed in stunned horror, for once jolted out of his cool aplomb. "Good Lord!" he swore beneath his breath. He looked up at Dominic, his gray eyes stricken. "I didn't know, Jake," he muttered. "I swear I didn't know. Why the hell didn't she tell me?"

"Because she's a stubborn young fool with more courage than sense," Jake said curtly. "I gather she was under the impression that you were trying to break her spirit." He shook his head in disgust. "I'd expect such behavior from a young firebrand like Jane, but what provoked you to go this far?"

Benjamin swallowed hard, looking slightly sick. "She may have been right. I don't know. She was so damned defiant that it got under my skin. Every day I thought she'd give in and ask me to change her duty, and every day she threw her refusal right back in my face." His hands came up to cover his eyes. "God, I feel rotten."

Jane felt her anger begin to drain away as she saw the unhappiness and self-reproach in Benjamin's face. She could grudgingly understand the irritation that had driven him to such lengths. Hadn't she been stirred by the same pride and stubbornness that had goaded the captain? She knew the same treacherous melting that she always experienced at the sight of another's distress or pain.

"I should think you would," Jake said scathingly. "You've acted with the same asinine stupidity that she has."

This remark was met with resentful scowls from both antagonists.

"It wasn't the captain's fault that I bruise easily," Jane said defensively, with an abrupt about-face. "You hired him to run your blasted ship for you. If he thought that I'd be of most value scrubbing decks, then that's what I should do." She scooted to the other end of the couch to evade Jake's reach and rose to her feet. "In fact, that's what I insist on doing!" she added emphatically. She turned and marched toward the door, brushing by the stunned captain with a curt nod. "I'll see you tomorrow morning at the usual time, Captain Benjamin."

The captain was having a predinner drink with Jake in the lounge one evening, shortly after they had sighted the northern coast of Mexico, and was mentally congratulating himself on his diplomatic brilliance. It appeared that his solution to the problem Jane had presented was working very well indeed in the past several days. His self-satisfaction in this respect was suddenly blasted into the stratosphere by a call from his first officer, Jim Davidson.

When he turned away from the phone, he grimaced as he picked up his whiskey. "I should have known that it was too good to last. That was Jim Davidson on the phone. It seems that we have a slight disciplinary problem with the crew. Five of them were caught shooting craps in the storeroom." He looked down gloomily at his drink. "One of them was your problem child, Jane Smith."

Jake Dominic lifted an eyebrow mockingly. "Surely that's not so reprehensible," he said easily. "You've always allowed the men to gamble on the *Sea Breeze*."

"Not for money," Benjamin said shortly. "Evidently there was quite a bit of cash involved in this particular game."

"I see," Jake replied thoughtfully; then his eyes lit mischievously. "And what discipline are you going to administer to these miscreants? Scrubbing the deck?"

"Lord, no!" Benjamin said with a shudder. "The men are easy enough to deal with. They know that the standard punishment for gambling is to stop their pay for a few days. But how in the hell do I discipline Jane, when she's not even earning a salary?"

Jake rose from the barstool and wandered over to the porthole to stare absently out at the tranquil sea that was just beginning to be stroked by the scarlet rays of the setting sun. "I'll take care of it." He spoke casually, over his shoulder. "As you say, she's my problem."

"I didn't think you'd want to be bothered," Benjamin said slowly. Though Dominic had inquired once or twice about Jane, he'd never once visited his charge in her cabin during the time that she'd been confined.

Jake Dominic turned around to face him, a sardonic smile on his face. "It would hardly have been discreet to display more than a casual interest in our little invalid. You know damn well if I'd paid so much as a courtesy call to Jane's cabin, the entire ship would have assumed that she was my mistress. The next two months are going to be difficult enough for her without that particular problem to deal with."

That Jake had been acting chivalrously to protect Jane had obviously never occurred to Benjamin. "So you haven't grown bored with your court jester yet," Benjamin remarked dryly. "That must be some kind of record for you, Jake."

He shrugged, his dark eyes shuttered. "She's an amusing child. I enjoy having her around." He smiled. "Even when she raises hell."

"Shall I tell Davidson to send her to you for discipline, then?" Benjamin asked slyly. "It wouldn't do to exempt her from punishment. It would set a bad precedent."

There was a trace of uneasiness in Jake's face. "It really wasn't a very serious offense," he suggested tentatively. Then, as Benjamin continued to stare at him implacably, he said in exasperation, "Oh, damn it to hell! Yes, send her to me. I'll think of something."

Benjamin smothered a smile as he turned away and once again lifted the receiver of the phone to give the order.

Jane arrived in the lounge five minutes later. She wore her own black jeans and a man's yellow sport shirt with the tails knotted under her small high breasts and the sleeves rolled up above the elbow. She also wore an expression of determination and defiance as she strode angrily into the room.

"It's utterly ridiculous for you to punish the men for having a friendly dice game," she cried furiously. She stopped before them, her breasts heaving, her flaming hair seeming to take additional fire from her blazing eyes. "It's absolutely medieval of you to withhold their pay for indulging in an innocent game on their own time!"

The two men exchanged amused glances before Benjamin attempted to assume a stern expression. "A game quite frequently ceases to be friendly when money is involved," he said coolly. "The rule is quite reasonable on shipboard. Men have been known to lose an entire month's salary when faced with their boredom of days at sea. Some of these men have wives and children to support at home. How would you like them to be in need, even hungry, because of a 'friendly' little dice game?"

Jane's eyes were wide and stricken. "I never thought of that," she said in a subdued tone. "You're quite right, of course."

"Of course," Benjamin agreed promptly. "However, we're here not to discuss the men's punishment, but your own, young lady. Not only have you disobeyed my orders about leaving your bed, but you've engaged in an illegal dice game."

Jane made a face. "My knees are almost entirely healed now, so there was no reason to stay in bed. It was driving me absolutely bananas. And I wasn't actually gambling. I didn't have any money, so Simon was just letting me throw out the dice for him."

"Simon?" Jake asked, his dark eyes narrowing.

"Your cousin, Simon." Jane said, surprised; then, as he continued to look puzzled, she quoted impishly: "Four times removed in blood, forty million dollars in substance."

"Oh, yes, Gordon Dominic's boy," Jake said dryly. "I'd forgotten that he was on board."

"You should get to know him better," Jane said with enthusiasm. "Simon is a super person."

"I'm glad you think so," Jake said tersely. "Personally, I don't think much of a man who involves a young girl in illegal gambling."

Benjamin raised his eyebrows at this hypocrisy from a man who had led dozens of women into much more iniquitous indiscretions, but he wisely withheld comment.

"It wasn't Simon's fault," Jane said staunchly. "He wouldn't even have been there himself, if I hadn't told him I had never seen a dice game and asked him to go with me."

"So it was you who lured the all-American boy down the path of wickedness," Jake said lazily, taking a swallow of his drink. "It did seem a little out of character, from what I remember of Simon."

"Couldn't you excuse him from punishment, just this time?" Jane pleaded wistfully. "It hardly seems fair that he should take the blame because I was curious."

"I can't understand your fascination," Jake remarked. "Surely a covert dice game in a deserted storeroom is a little on the sordid side."

"Well, actually it was rather exciting," Jane said with a reminiscent smile. "You see, I'd never seen anyone gamble before. My grandfather was very strict about things like that."

"I can't make an exception in Simon's case," Benjamin said emphatically. "Any more than we can in your own." He turned to Jake. "Have you made a decision as to her punishment?"

A curious smile lit Jake Dominic's dark face as he stared with narrowed eyes into Jane's. "Oh, yes, I think so," he drawled. "Where's the closest gambling casino, Marc?"

Benjamin answered warily, "San Miguel. It's a few miles down the coast." His eyes narrowed as he saw the flickering devilment in the other man's expression.

"Good," Jake said with satisfaction. "I've thought

it over, Marc, and what Jane needs isn't discipline, but knowledge. We need to show her the wickedness of these games of chance so that she may satisfy her curiosity and get it out of her system."

"Rather an unusual solution," Benjamin said sardonically. "So you intend to take her to San Miguel tonight." It was a statement, not a question.

Jake nodded, his eyes still on Jane's face, which had suddenly come alive with excitement. "I feel it my duty," he said mockingly. "Care to come along, Marc?"

"I think I'd better," Benjamin said grimly. "San Miguel isn't Monte Carlo, you know. It's little more than a dive. It's certainly not the type of place you'd take a lady."

"Well, we can take care of that easily enough," Jake replied, his eyes running over Jane's slight figure. "Just find her a loose coat and that stocking cap she had on when she burgled my cabin. The lights are bound to be dim in the casino, and she'll have no trouble passing as a boy."

"I'll wear the white sweater Simon lent me," Jane put in eagerly. "I'm lost in it."

"Just the thing," he agreed promptly, his lips twitching.

"Should I bind my breasts?" Jane asked worriedly, looking down at her feminine roundness with profound disapproval.

Jake made a sound between a cough and a gasp. "No, I don't think that will be necessary," he said solemnly, not looking at her. "Why don't you run along and get into your disguise? Meet us on deck in thirty minutes."

"Right," Jane agreed happily, and ran from the lounge.

Jake released the whoop of laughter that he'd been suppressing. He bent over the bar, his shoulders shaking helplessly with mirth.

Captain Benjamin looked on in disapproval. "I'm glad you're so entertained," he said caustically. "You know that this isn't a wise venture, Jake."

Still chuckling, Jake commented, "Sometimes being wise can be abysmally dull, Marc. I can't wait to see her reaction to San Miguel."

Benjamin frowned. "I don't like the idea of exposing a girl to that kind of atmosphere just to furnish you with a few kicks, Jake."

"She'll be safe enough with both of us there to protect her." Jake said carelessly. "Jane's wild to go. You saw her face."

The captain nodded reluctantly. "I can't deny that. But damn it, she doesn't have the best track record for choosing what's good for her!"

"Why, Marc, you sound positively fatherly."

"The girl needs someone to take care of her. And neither of us has the qualifications for the job."

Jake slapped him on the shoulder. "For heaven's sake, Marc," he said impatiently, "we're not adopting the girl; we're only taking her out." He swallowed the rest of his drink and set his glass on the bar. "Now, while I go down and change, why don't you run along and check to make sure Jane's not doing something drastic?"

"Drastic?" Benjamin asked, puzzled.

Jake Dominic's eyes danced. "She seemed very concerned about looking like a boy." He grinned. "What's more girlish than a woman's crowning glory?"

"Crowning glo—you mean her hair?" Benjamin asked, his eyes widening. "You think she'd cut off all her hair?"

"It wouldn't surprise me," Jake said mildly.

"Oh, my God!" Benjamin exclaimed, and he bolted from the room.

Five

The casino was located at the top of a hill overlooking the dusty, picturesque port town of San Miguel. The trip up the winding dirt road proved only a short ten minutes in the ancient rattling taxi that Jake Dominic had magically produced at the dock, and they were soon pulling into a bumpy, unpaved parking lot.

Jane peered eagerly out the window, her golden eyes blazing with curiosity and excitement. The parking lot was crowded even this early in the evening, she noticed. The large one-story prefab building that housed the casino was painted an astounding flamingo pink, and the name Tropicana was blazoned in nauseating chartreuse over the double doors at the front entrance.

"Disappointed?" Jake asked lazily, when she made no comment.

Jane shook her head. "Oh, no," she said positively. "It's just as I imagined a dive would look." She frowned in puzzlement. "Except for all those lights." Both the front and rear of the casino were lit by several brilliant streetlights that illuminated the area until it was almost as bright as daylight.

He shrugged. "At a place like this it's probably

necessary if you don't want to come back to a car with no tires."

Benjamin nodded in agreement. "I've seen thieves completely strip a car inside and out in ten minutes," he said dryly. "And that was in downtown Mexico City!"

Instructing the taxi driver to wait and insuring his compliance with a sizeable monetary exchange, Jake ushered them leisurely from the car, through the double doors, and into the crowded, smoky interior of the casino.

"It's utterly fantastic," Jane breathed ecstatically. "It's like the movie set from *Casablanca*."

Jake flinched. "Please," he protested, with a pained expression. "Rick's Place at least had a certain class. This is more like the cantina scene from *Duel in the Sun*."

The entire far wall of the room was occupied by a long narrow bar. The rest of the large room was furnished with several green baize tables, offering various games of chance. The dimly lit room was crowded and noisy even this early in the evening. The patrons were almost exclusively male, for the most part Mexicans, dressed in dark trousers and the ubiquitous long white shirts and sandals.

The exception to the masculine atmosphere was provided by several voluptuously endowed *señoritas* in low-cut scarlet gowns who were presiding as dealers at the gaming tables. The old-fashioned ceiling fans served only to shift the smoke-laden air rather than freshen it, and the faces of the gamblers were shining with perspiration as they crowded close to the tables as if magnetized by the red-gowned dealers.

"Stay close to either Marc or me," Jake ordered. "And keep that cap pulled down!"

Jane nodded eagerly, jamming her hands in the pockets of the oversized jacket Captain Benjamin had provided, and swaggered after the two men with what she hoped was a boyish gait. Jake and Benjamin's goal was the crowded roulette table where Benjamin elbowed a place for Jane. Marc Benjamin and Jake swiftly purchased chips from a dark-haired beauty, who gave them a dazzling smile, and they preceeded to play for several minutes, with indifferent success.

"Would you like to try your luck?" Jake asked quietly, pushing some chips in front of her.

Jane shook her head. "I'd rather watch." The excitement and tension on the faces of the players was infinitely more interesting to her than winning or losing.

Jake shrugged. "It's really not my game either," he said, looking around restlessly. "I think I'll try to find a blackjack table. Do you want to come with me?"

"No, I'll stay here with Captain Benjamin," Jane said absently, her eyes on an obese man whose good luck was being raucously celebrated by much back-slapping and shouting. She was vaguely aware of Dominic's withdrawal.

For perhaps an hour she continued to watch with undiminished interest the goings-on at the roulette table before she, too, became restless. She looked down the table at Benjamin, hoping that he would also be ready to move on to another table. He looked quite content, however, his eyes fixed intently on the spinning wheel and a large stack of chips in front of him. He was winning heavily and would probably not even notice that she'd gone, she decided. She hadn't received more than a passing glance from any of the clientele of the casino. It should be safe enough for her to drift around by herself for a while.

She faded away from the table and pushed her way through to the sidelines to decide where to go next. She spotted a dice table in the corner of the room and decided to start there. For the next thirty minutes she visited several tables, with gradually dwindling interest. It was with some relief and pleasure that she finally spotted Dominic at a table across the room.

Jane started forward eagerly, only to stop abruptly after a few paces. The game Jake Dominic was playing was not confined to the cards in front of him. The ravishing Mexican dealer was leaning toward him with an unmistakable glint of invitation in her dark eyes as she murmured something to him that brought a cynical smile to his lips and a look of appraisal to his eyes. His eyes wandered leisurely over the woman's generous curves, lingering for a long moment on the cleavage that was blatantly displayed in the low-cut gown, before he gave the woman an answer that made her smile with sultry contentment.

Jane felt a stab of pain so intense that it took her breath away. For a moment she stood there, her emotions raw and confused, before her mind clamped a protective shield over the hurt and started to provide her with a rationalization for that revealing moment of agony.

Of course she had felt something when she'd seen Jake with that woman, she told herself. They had grown so close in the companionable evenings alone together that she knew a certain sense of possession. It was natural that she would feel a trifle bereft when Dominic showed the unmistakable signs of desire for another, even though the relationship he was contemplating with the sexy woman was far different from the casual friendship he had with Jane. She should have known that a virile man of Jake Dominic's reputation would immediately seek out a woman willing to satisfy his desires when the opportunity presented itself. It had been surprise, not pain, that had shaken her in that first moment, she told herself firmly.

She turned away, carefully avoiding looking at the intimacy of the couple at the blackjack table. Jake would not welcome a third party at this stage, she thought unhappily. Abruptly all pleasure was drained from the evening, and the scene that had been fascinating a few minutes before was now merely sordid.

She drifted over to the sidelines again, and leaned against the wall to watch the action in the smoky room with only casual interest. She was conscious now of the heat of the room. Her sweater and the loose coat that enveloped her were stifling, and she could feel a bead of perspiration form at the nape of her neck.

Her gaze ran casually around the room and then stopped abruptly. There was a small, nearly hidden door at the far end of the long, mirrored bar, which she had overlooked in her first glance around the room. It obviously led outside to the rear of the building, and as she looked, a steady stream of gamblers wandered through the door. None ever returned, though she watched carefully for another ten minutes. Her curiosity was irresistibly piqued.

She straightened slowly and moved forward, her gaze fixed in fascination on that mysterious door.

Jake Dominic looked indifferently at the card the Mexican woman had just dealt him, before lifting his eyes to gaze with slightly more appreciation at the generous cleavage revealed by the dealer's low-cut gown. Then his forehead creased in a puzzled frown when his glance passed from those pleasant pastures to drift restlessly about the room. The crowd had thinned now, and he could see Benjamin, still at the roulette table. But where the devil was Jane?

Suddenly there was a loud commotion at the far end of the bar as a short, stocky Mexican came bursting through the door shouting something to the bartender and waving his arms wildly. The bartender grabbed a baseball bat from under the bar and ran out the door, followed closely by the man who had summoned him.

Jake hurriedly threw his cards on the table and had crossed the room to the roulette table in seconds.

He grabbed Marc Benjamin by the arm and asked tersely, "Where the hell is Jane?"

"I thought she was with you," Benjamin said, surprised.

Jake had a chill of foreboding as he remembered the brilliant lights that surrounded the casino. The lights in the parking lot were self-explanatory, but what about the lighting in the rear?

He reached across the table and grasped the dealer's arm as she reached out to take in the house's winnings. "That door by the bar," he asked urgently. "Where does it lead?"

The woman shrugged her bare shoulders. *"Pelea de gallos,"* she answered indifferently.

"Pelea de gallos!" He started for the door at a dead run. "Cockfight!" he shouted over his shoulder to Benjamin, and heard a violent exclamation. The captain caught up with him as Jake went through the door.

The scene that greeted their eyes was a wild melee of shouting, angry Mexicans who had left their wooden spectator benches and gathered around the pit arena in the center of the clearing. The object of their rage seemed to be the small figure lying on the hard-packed dirt in the center of the arena who was virtually covered by the bodies of several furious men, their fists swinging as they competed with one another in their attempts to do the worst possible damage to the red-haired gringo beneath them.

"My God! It's Jane!" Jake breathed, and without thinking he dashed forward, pushing and shoving through the crowd till he reached the pile of bodies. Lifting and pulling the men off her with frantic strength, he finally uncovered the dust- and blood-covered body of Jane Smith clutching a huge glossy black cock in her arms in a deathlike grip.

"Are you all right?" he shouted as he warded off a punch to his midsection from a burly man who didn't appreciate having his revenge thwarted.

Jane nodded as she got shakily to her knees and then to her feet, while Jake and Marc Benjamin, on either side of her, kept the crowd back by the primitive but effective method of punching whatever vulnerable spot on their antagonists' bodies presented itself.

"Let's get out of here!" Jake shouted, as he saw the bartender with the baseball bat edging closer.

They each grabbed one of Jane's arms and rushed forward, knocking heads and punching faces indiscriminately as they progressed slowly across the clearing to the side of the building. When they broke clear of the crowd, they ran desperately for the waiting taxi, with a stream of shouting men hard on their heels.

They reached the taxi and piled hurriedly into the back seat. Jake shouted, *"Vamanos!"* in such a commanding voice that the startled taxi driver immediately reversed the car with a screech of tires, almost running over the first vanguard of their pursuers.

This resulted in another burst of threatening curses and fist shaking, as the driver sped out of the parking lot with his foot jammed down on the accelerator and his frightened eyes on the angry mob in his rearview mirror. He continued to drive with breakneck speed down the hill, half muttering prayers for himself and half curses against the crazy gringos who had gotten him into this.

Jake turned to Jane, his expression grim. "My God, you've still got that damn cock," he said disgustedly, looking with disfavor at the beady-eyed bird in Jane's arms. "I gather that revolting creature is the reason for all this?"

Jane nodded, her breathing gradually steadying. "It was terrible." She shuddered, her golden eyes darkening to topaz at the memory. "Those horrible men were making them fight with those hideous spurs on their feet. They were bleeding and hurt and nobody cared. I tried to make them stop, but they wouldn't listen."

"So you grabbed one of the birds in the ring to assure that they would," Benjamin surmised, shaking his head incredulously.

"It was the only thing I could do," she explained simply. "But it made them awfully angry."

"I can imagine," Jake said dryly. "A good bit of money rides on those birds."

"Well, I'm glad I did it," Jane said defiantly. "They were wrong to be so cruel."

"There are thousands of people doing cruel things in this world," Jake said caustically. "Are you going to try to right all their wrongs?"

Her eyes filled with tears. "I had to do it," she repeated huskily.

"Do you know that you almost got yourself killed back there?" Jake asked through clenched teeth.

"Leave her alone, Jake," Marc said with rough kindness. "She's had enough for one night."

"I could break her neck," Jake said savagely, his gaze taking in her bruised and bleeding lip and her left eye, which was darkening rapidly. "Just look at her, damn it."

Jane shrank back against the solid shoulder of the captain. When she spoke, her lips trembled pitifully. "I'm sorry," she apologized miserably. "I didn't mean to cause any trouble."

"You *are* trouble," Jake said tersely as the taxi pulled up at the dock where the launch waited.

He jumped out of the taxi and half assisted, half jerked Jane out of the car. He reached into his pocket and pulled out several bills, which he handed to the driver with a curt *"Gracias."* The taxi driver's glower turned to a broad smile as he saw the size of the bills. He touched the brim of his wide straw hat in a respectful salute and drove off with a triumphant roar.

Meanwhile, Marc Benjamin had exited from the other door and had lithely jumped down into the launch and started the motor.

As Jake lifted Jane into the boat, the captain asked, above the low throb of the engine, "You're not going to let her take that cock on the *Sea Breeze*, surely?"

"What the hell do you suggest we do with it?" Jake asked bitterly. "Toss it into the sea? Jane would probably dive in after it."

"We could always give it to your chef and see what he could do with it," Marc drawled wryly. "It would certainly be a challenge to his expertise."

"No!" Jane cried, shocked. "You wouldn't." Her arms tightened protectively around the rooster.

"Of course we wouldn't," Jake said disgustedly. "He's joking, for heaven's sake." He turned to Benjamin. "Get us back to the *Sea Breeze*, Marc, or, so help me, I may toss them both into the sea!"

When they arrived back at the yacht, they were assisted aboard by a surprised and curious young seaman who tried not to stare too obviously at the disreputable-looking trio. Both Jake and Marc showed the signs of the violent free-for-all they'd been engaged in. Jake sported a bruise on his cheekbone that was rapidly turning a livid purple, and Benjamin's usually immaculate uniform jacket was torn raggedly from the lapel to the shoulder seam.

Jake carefully took the cock from Jane's arms and handed it to the seaman. "Be careful of the spurs," he cautioned, ignoring the man's dumbfounded expression. "Take him down to the storeroom and give him feed and water."

"I'll do it," Jane offered. "He's my responsibility."

"The hell you will," Jake said annoyedly. "You're coming down to my cabin so that I can have a look at those bruises. Coming, Marc?"

Marc Benjamin shook his head ruefully. "I'd better go to my own cabin and make some repairs. I'll be along later."

Jake nodded briefly and, taking Jane by the elbow, propelled her ahead of him, leaving the seaman to look after them, wondering blankly what the devil one fed a fighting cock.

Jake opened the door of his cabin and pushed her ahead of him into the room, flipping on the lights as he did so. Jane looked around her with interest. The night of her intrusion, she'd had no opportunity to appreciate the beauty of the master cabin. The thick carpet, she noted, was a silver gray, as were the shades on the bedside lamps. The spread that graced the king-sized bed was black velvet. The simple, elegant decor was oddly ascetic, considering its owner's worldliness. The only glaring note in the understated richness of the cabin was her own graffiti scribbled on the wall across from the bed.

Jane winced. "Can't you cover that up until you can have the panel replaced?" she asked.

Jake followed her glance and shrugged. "Marc offered to have his men make some temporary repairs, but I told him to leave it alone. I'm learning to live with it."

He strode into the bathroom, pulling her along with him. Once there, he lifted her onto the vanity counter while he rummaged in the medicine cabinet for unguentine and iodine.

"This isn't really necessary, you know," Jane said gently, watching his lean, taut face. "I'm sure you and Captain Benjamin took more punishment than I did. Those crazy men were hitting one another more than they were hitting me."

"How very comforting," Jake jeered. "So instead of broken bones and internal injuries, you only have severe cuts and bruises." Despite the anger in his voice, his hands were incredibly gentle as he washed the cut on her lip with a cold cloth. "At the rate you're going, you'll be lucky if you live to be twenty-one."

She smiled tremulously. "I promise that I'll be more careful in the future," she said lightly. "At least until the cruise is over. I fully intend to make sure you get your money's worth in labor to pay for that panel."

"Damn the panel!" Jake spoke harshly, his black eyes flaming. "Do you have any idea what would have happened if that mob in the pit tonight had discovered that you were a woman?"

Her golden eyes flew to his face in bewilderment. "You mean . . ." she whispered, and blushed uncontrollably. "But they were so angry. . . ."

"My God, Jane!" Jake said savagely. "Anger can be as much of an aphrodisiac as any other stimulant. Don't you know that?"

She shook her head, her eyes suddenly frightened. "No, I didn't know that," she answered simply.

"It figures," he said shortly. "For a girl who's lived all over the world, you've picked up relatively little common sense. That grandfather of yours must have kept you tied up."

"Everything happened too fast," she replied defensively. "I didn't have time to think and analyze every movement I made. I just knew that I had to stop them before they killed those two birds."

Jake carefully applied iodine to the cut lip before answering. His tone was grim. "I should have chained you to my wrist before I took you into that place."

Jane dropped her eyes. "You would have found that a trifle inconvenient," she said obscurely, remembering the sultry beauty at the blackjack table.

His eyes narrowed. "What's that supposed to mean?" he asked, critically examining her eye. "You're going to have a beaut of a shiner," he commented.

"Nothing," Jane murmured, as he tilted her chin and dabbed gently with the cold cloth at her swollen eye.

"You should never try to lie, redhead," he said dryly. "You're clear as glass. Now, answer me."

"It's just that I saw you with that woman," Jane said awkwardly. "I'm sorry if my getting into trouble interrupted you."

"What woman?" Jake asked, puzzled. Then his eyes gleamed mischievously. "Oh, that woman." He threw the cloth into the sink and uncapped the small jar of unguentine and started smoothing the salve around her eye. "We hadn't reached the point where an interruption would have caused me any really traumatic frustration."

Jane felt a rush of inexplicable relief at the knowledge that he had obviously forgotten the woman existed until she mentioned her.

"She was very beautiful," Jane said tentatively.

"Luscious, quite luscious," he agreed absently.. Then he grinned mockingly. "What are you hinting at, brat? Are you under the same impression as Marc, that I can't survive the cruise without a woman in my bed?"

"Well, you do have that reputation," Jane said

demurely, her golden eyes dancing, "but you seem to be holding up very well, for a satyr."

"You know, I'm tempted to make that black eye into a matched set," he said in a conversational tone. "Not only do you deprive me of sexual solace, but you have the supreme insolence to taunt me with it."

She giggled, and he flashed her a smile of such warmth that her heart skipped a beat. "Laugh, will you?" he said with mock ferocity. "I ought to make you take the luscious Consuelo's place in my bed tonight."

She made a face. "You're not that hard up," she said with an impudent grin.

"Well, it would be a bit like taking a prize fighter to bed," he granted dryly. "But you know how we satyrs are—anybody would do in a clinch," he punned.

She groaned. "That's terrible, Jake. I think I'd prefer the black eye."

He grinned unrepentantly. "You're lucky I can still joke after a night like this one. For a while it was a draw whether the mob would kill you before I did."

"Oh, my God, I haven't thanked you!" she gasped, horrified. "You and Captain Benjamin probably saved my life, and I didn't even tell you how much I appreciate it."

"You were a little busy at the time," Jake said mockingly. "For that matter, so were Marc and I."

"And you were hurt," she cried remorsefully, her fingers gently touching the bruise on his cheekbone. Impulsively she reached up and pressed a fairy-light kiss on the bruised flesh. Then she drew back in a panic of shyness.

There was a curious flicker deep in Jake Dominic's eyes, but his voice was light. "Do you always kiss to make well? It's not a half-bad idea. Perhaps I'll try it."

His hands slowly reached up and cradled her face tenderly. She forgot to breathe as she stared wide-eyed up into the dark intentness of his eyes. "Shut your eyes, brat," he said huskily. "I'm about to conduct a medical experiment."

She obediently closed her eyes, and was immediately rewarded with a kiss on the lips that wooed and caressed like the first gentle breath of spring. It was followed by a butterfly kiss on the closed lid of her bruised eye and then another, just as light, on the other lid.

"That eye wasn't hurt," she protested dreamily, lifting her face like a flower to the sun.

"Stop complaining," Jake ordered. "I threw that one in for balance." His lips brushed the tip of her nose with infinite gentleness. "Now, is there anyplace that I've missed? I'm completely at your disposal."

Jane slowly opened her eyes, feeling almost drugged by the honey sweetness of the moment. She felt as if he had wrapped her in a silken protective cloak of warmth and affection and irresistible tenderness.

Jake's face was close, only a breath away, his black eyes laughing into her own. Then suddenly the laughter was gone and his eyes held something else in their flickering depths. Something that charged the atmosphere with electricity and caused the blood to race in her veins as if she'd been running a marathon race. She felt radiantly alive and at the same time languidly dreamy.

"Jane," Jake said huskily, his flickering eyes mesmerizing her with their dark flames.

"What's happening?" Jane whispered breathlessly, feeling suddenly as if she were captured in a melting pool of sensation whose nucleus was the intent face and virile body of the man before her. "What's happening to us, Jake?"

The words ripped the gossamer spell that surrounded them. Dominic drew a deep breath, and his eyes became shuttered and impenetrable. His hands dropped from her face, and his mouth twisted in familiar mockery.

"That, my innocent little nitwit, is what is known as *chemistry*. Or to put it more succinctly—sex. For a moment, there, you looked pretty good to me despite that black eye."

"You looked pretty good to me, too," she said quietly, her eyes shining serenely.

Jake shook his head wonderingly. "They shouldn't let you run around loose," he said flatly. "Didn't anyone ever tell you that you shouldn't say things like that to a man like me? God, you'd be a pushover for a man who was really on the make."

Jane's eyes filled with tears at the cynicism in his voice. "So I'm stupid," she said huskily. "I'm not like you. I can't hide what I'm feeling. I wouldn't want to."

She tried to slip off the vanity counter, but he stopped her with his hands on her shoulders. "I know," he said resignedly. "Like I said, clear as glass. It's time you learned to put up a few defenses, Jane."

She looked at him thoughtfully for a moment, then slowly shook her head. "You don't mean defenses, you mean armor," she said quietly. "I couldn't live like that. Hiding behind a shield because I was afraid to reach out and touch someone."

"There is a middle road, you know," Jake observed.

"Not for me."

Jake Dominic studied her determined face and clear, steady eyes for a long moment. He lifted her gently down from the vanity. "No, not for you," he agreed quietly. "And may God help you, redhead!"

He touched her cheek gently with one long finger, before he turned away and said briskly, "I believe a dose of remedial whiskey is in order. I'll call Marc and tell him to meet us in the lounge."

Six

Jane woke up too late to have breakfast the next morning, having opted to sleep for a precious thirty minutes more, after her late night. As this was the first morning of her training as cook's help for Sam Brockmeyer and she did not want to be late, she was half running when she came up on deck.

Simon Dominic hailed her cheerfully and fell into step with her. He noted the black eye and cut lip with frank curiosity. "What a shiner!"

Jane made a face at him. "You should have seen the other guys," she loftily. "I should have known that our little adventure would have been all over the ship by this time. And they say women are gossips!"

Simon grinned. "Well, you can't show up with a fighting cock in your arms, and the three of you looking as if you'd been in a barroom brawl, without exciting a little curiosity."

"I can't tell you about it now," Jane said briskly. "I don't want to start off on the wrong foot with Mr. Brockmeyer by being late."

Simon gave her an understanding look. "I'll see you at dinner and help you lick your wounds. There may be even more of them by then. Brockmeyer is a terror to work for."

"Don't worry. I cut my teeth on top sergeants," Jane said flippantly. "You only have to remember to get in the first punch." Ignoring Simon's answering chuckle, she broke into a brisk sprint in the direction of the kitchen.

She had only a moment to appreciate the stainless-steel cleanliness of Brockmeyer's domain, before a voice bellowed menacingly from the planning desk in the far corner of the room. "You're late!"

This was patently untrue, as could be seen by the large clock on the wall. Jane moved forward serenely to stand before the cluttered desk and forebore apologizing, which the arch demon of the *Sea Breeze* obviously expected of her.

"Good morning, Mr. Brockmeyer," she said cheerfully. "I'm Jane Smith. I'm looking forward to working with you."

Sam Brockmeyer was a tall, lanky man in his late thirties, with a slightly receding hairline and the creased, jowly face of a mournful bloodhound. His soft brown eyes should have been appealing, but there was nothing endearing about the stony glare that the chef was directing at her.

"And I thought they had given me the dregs before," he said scathingly, his eyes running distastefully over her battered face and diminutive figure, in its oversized garments. "You must be Captain Benjamin's final revenge."

Jane smiled at him sunnily. "No, actually I'm your reward for being such a brilliant chef," she said sweetly. "My grandfather hated poor food, and since we often lived in less civilized corners of the world, he had me trained in Paris. Naturally, I'm not up to your standards, but I think you'll find I'm adequate." She paused. "I think you can teach me a good deal more, and I'm not about to be intimidated by your shouting or slave driving. Do we understand each other?"

Brockmeyer stared at her for a long moment, his face impassive, before saying slowly, "We understand each other, Miss Smith." He gave her a toothy grin.

In the next four days Brockmeyer appeared to be trying to make her eat those brave words. If Jane had not been absolutely sincere in what she had told the chef, he would have terrorized her, as he had her predecessors. Jane found herself working ceaselessly from six in the morning until nine at night in an atmosphere of turbulence that made a tropical hurricane appear as gentle as a summer breeze. The slightest clumsiness or mistake was met with a virulent diatribe from Brockmeyer's scourging tongue, and he obviously was taking malicious pleasure in singling out Jane for attention.

Jane accepted both the exhausting labor and verbal abuse with a cheerful serenity that frequently brought a look of baffled frustration to the chef's face. Though only allowed to do the donkey's work to begin with, Jane was gradually permitted minor cooking tasks. She made it her business to be in the general area when Brockmeyer was cooking, in order to observe the master at work.

Brockmeyer considered himself personally responsible for lunch and dinner for the crew and all of Jake Dominic's meals. The meals for the crew, since they were presented cafeteria-style, were less elaborate, but Brockmeyer still insisted that they be excellent. The meals prepared for Dominic were epicurean delights.

Jane gradually became aware that her hard work and uncomplaining attitude were earning Brockmeyer's grudging respect. This fact was brought home to her when a mistake by Ralph, the steward, who was entrusted with serving Dominic's lunch, threw Brockmeyer into a towering rage.

"What's the fool trying to do to me?" Brockmeyer howled, his spaniel eyes shooting fire. "I make Trout Almondine and the idiot serves red wine! I'll strangle him with my bare hands!"

As the guilty party had discreetly vanished at the first blistering words, this was not very likely to happen. However, Jane and the other kitchen minions busily went about their own tasks knowing that any word would immediately bring the chef's wrath down upon their own heads.

"How can I be expected to tolerate these blunderheads?" he raged, storming to the phone and dialing rapidly. Jane could not hear what he said and was quite surprised when a frowning Marcus Benjamin strode into the kitchen. Jane hid a smile. So even the captain was not immune to Brockmeyer's autocracy.

"I won't use that ass of a steward again!" Brockmeyer declared explosively as soon as Benjamin walked in the door.

Benjamin shrugged. "So I'll assign you another one," he said soothingly.

"And have the same thing happen again?" Brockmeyer asked caustically, "Your men are all ignorant philistines where fine cuisine is concerned."

"They're all good seaman," Benjamin said. "Ralph's mistake was surely minor."

"Minor!" Brockmeyer roared, "You call red wine with Trout Almondine minor?"

"Well, perhaps—"

"It will not happen again," Brockmeyer interrupted. "You'll assign her as Dominic's steward." He punched a finger in Jane's direction.

Jane almost dropped the potato she was peeling. She looked up, her eyes wide and startled.

Benjamin looked equally startled. "You want her out of your kitchen?" he asked slowly. "I suppose that I could change her duty assignment again."

"I didn't say that," Brockmeyer snapped. "She's adequate at her job."

Jane grinned happily at this grudging admission, which was the equivalent of the highest praise.

"She can be excused from her kitchen duties long enough to attend to Mr. Dominic. At least she can't be worse than those other idiots you sent me."

"Then it's done," Benjamin consented, relieved. He turned to go, obviously eager to escape.

"Just a moment," Brockmeyer said. "We're not finished." He waved a hand at Jane. "Look at her.

Just the sight of her is enough to put anyone off his food. Even my food. You must get her out of those monstrosities she's wearing, before tomorrow. Do you understand?"

"We happen to be at sea," Benjamin reminded him dryly, "or didn't that occur to you?"

"That's your problem," Brockmeyer said tersely. "I won't have her serving my meals looking like a ragpicker."

"I'll speak to Mr. Dominic," Benjamin said, "but I can't promise anything." He turned and left the kitchen.

Whatever the tenor of Benjamin's conversation with Dominic, that evening the *Sea Breeze* anchored off the tiny port town of San Juárez. The next morning a launch was sent to pick up a number of packages that had been flown there, first by jet and then by helicopter, from Mexico City.

When Brockmeyer piled the packages into Jane's arms a few moments after they were delivered by launch to the *Sea Breeze*, he had a grimly triumphant smile on his face.

"You'd best check to see if they fit," he said gruffly. "You'll be serving lunch today."

Jane hurried happily to her cabin, more excited by the gift of these garments than she could ever remember being before. It wasn't surprising, she thought wryly, after tripping around in clothes that made her look like the second banana in a vaudeville show.

She hurriedly ripped off the heavy expensive wrapping paper on the packages and stared blissfully at her treasures. There was not only a handsome steward's uniform much like Simon's, but also several pairs of designer jeans, blouses, sweaters, a swimsuit, a nightgown, low-heeled shoes, and bras and panties. There was even a lavish makeup kit.

For the next twenty minutes Jane tried on everything that she had received, with a growing appreciation for the person who had ordered her new wardrobe. Everything fit perfectly. Someone had a very good eye, and she rather suspected that that someone was Jake Dominic. After all, he had probably had a lot of experience in buying clothing for his women.

When Jane finally donned the uniform, she was more than pleased with the result. The white polyester slacks were a perfect fit, as was the white turtleneck blouse. The caramel-beige waist-length jacket gave her rather the appearance of a bellboy, but it also fit beautifully, and the color went well with her hair, she noticed, pleased. She added a touch of peach gloss to her lips and brushed her hair until it gleamed. It was amazing what a little lipstick could do for the morale. For the first time in nearly three weeks, she felt truly feminine.

No, not the first time, she thought, remembering that dizzying moment in Jake Dominic's cabin when she had felt more a woman than she had at any time in her life. She dismissed the thought firmly, and hurriedly put away her new things in the small teak chest before returning to the kitchen for her final instructions from Sam Brockmeyer.

Brockmeyer had informed her that unless Mr. Dominic had a large party of guests aboard, he preferred to have his meals served in the lounge. Though the surroundings were casual, Brockmeyer's table arrangements were not. It took Jane a full thirty minutes to set up the table in the elegant manner the chef felt his creations deserved, and then to transfer the meal in specially heated trays from the kitchen to the lounge. She then carefully chose a suitable bottle of wine from the wine rack behind the bar and moved briskly to stand beside the table.

Jake Dominic entered the lounge a few minutes later, and his brows shot up in amusement as he noted Jane's almost military stance. "For heaven's sake, relax! You make me feel like the prince in a comic opera."

Jane shot him an indignant glance but remained at attention. He looked like a prince, she thought with a little tingle of awareness. The dark prince

Lucifer dressed in fitted black jeans and a black long-sleeve sport shirt. Jane had not seen him since she had started her duties with Brockmeyer, and she stifled the unreasoning surge of pleasure at the sight of that dark face.

"I have my instructions, sir," she said sedately, as he strolled to his chair. She was immediately behind it and ready to seat him.

He frowned threateningly. "You do that and I'll smack that pert little bottom, brat."

Jane's face drooped with disappointment, but she obediently moved back to her former position and poured the wine with a little flourish. His crooked eyebrow rose mockingly as she uncovered the soup and set it carefully before him.

"You're overplaying it, Jane," he said dryly, picking up his spoon. "Why don't you pull up a chair and join me?"

Her eyes widened. "Oh, I couldn't," she answered, shocked. "Mr. Brockmeyer would be positively furious."

"And I will be equally furious if I have an attack of indigestion from all this hovering," he said silkily. "Sit down!"

She reluctantly drew up a chair and perched on it gingerly, her face stormy. "You're not being fair. I'm only trying to do my duties properly," she said. "You wouldn't invite Ralph to sit down and have lunch with you."

"The same rules don't apply," he said coolly. "I wouldn't threaten to smack Ralph's bottom, either." Ignoring her sudden rush of color, he commented casually, "That uniform fits very well. I thought it would."

This confirmed her earlier suspicion, and she said gratefully, "Everything fits beautifully. Thank you."

Jake shrugged, his eyes gleaming wickedly. "Personally, I was growing rather fond of your Orphan Annie image," he drawled. "But it was either garb you decently or court ptomaine poisoning for the remainder of the cruise. How did you tame our Tiger of the Kitchen in just four days?"

"Mr. Brockmeyer is not a tiger," she protested stoutly. Then, meeting his skeptical look, she conceded, "Well, if he is, he has good reason to be. He's totally dedicated to his work and is a great artist. It's no wonder that he's so difficult. Just look at his background." She paused for effect. "He was born in Cleveland!"

Jake took a sip of his wine and said solemnly, "How very unfortunate." There was a suspicious twitch to his lips as he added, "I suppose that does have some significance, but I can't quite grasp it."

"Well, of course, it does," Jane said impatiently. "Whoever heard of a great chef from Cleveland, Ohio? The entire restaurant world is prejudiced in favor of French chefs. Even Italian chefs are given more opportunities than Americans." She leaned forward, warming to her subject, her cheeks flushed. "I read an article in *Gourmet* magazine a few years ago about Sam Brockmeyer. Do you know that, as great as he is, he wasn't able to get work in any four-star restaurant in the world until he assumed the name of Pierre LeClaire?" Her voice rose indignantly. "Why, he even had to fake a French accent to get his first prestigious job! Can you imagine what that would do to a man of his temperament?"

Jake was grinning unashamedly now, his ebony eyes dancing. "I can see that a delicate flower like Brockmeyer could suffer irreparable psychological damage."

Jane smiled reluctantly. "Well, he is a brilliant artist. He must be very sensitive under that gruff exterior."

Jake's smile was cynical. "It doesn't naturally follow. I'm considered rather brilliant myself in some circles, and I assure you that I'm as hard as nails."

She shook her head, her face troubled. "Don't say that. You couldn't be that tough and still be so kind to me. I'd probably be behind bars now if you were."

"Don't make the mistake of putting me on a

pedestal, redhead," he corrected her wryly. "I'm a selfish bastard, and I always do exactly as I please. If I'd been in a different mood that night, I'd have turned you over to the authorities without a second thought."

"I don't believe that," Jane said quietly, her eyes steady on his.

"Then you're a fool," he replied softly, his dark eyes ruthless. "Ask Marc what kind of man I am."

Jane's gaze dropped. "I trust my own judgment," she insisted stubbornly.

"You'll forgive me if I fail to be impressed by your efforts in that area to date. Well, I've warned you, Jane, and that's more than I've done for any other woman. Just don't expect me to be better than I am."

"I don't think you know what you can be," she said daringly. "Or who you really are."

Jake's lips tightened, and his black eyes flickered. "And you do, I suppose," he remarked caustically.

Jane shook her head hesitantly. "Not yet," she said quietly, "but I'm beginning to think I may soon."

The look he bestowed on her was half angry, half amused, before the impenetrable shutter once more masked his expression. "You'd better pray that the final unveiling doesn't scare the hell out of you, redhead," he said lightly.

He reached for the bottle of wine and filled another glass and handed it to her. "Now, if you won't join me for lunch, at least have a glass of wine," he ordered, grinning mischievously. "I promise I won't tell Brockmeyer."

A few mornings later, they anchored at a small island off the southern coast of Mexico in answer to an urgent radio message from one Sheik Ahmet Kahlid, a Middle Eastern oil potentate and apparently an old friend of Dominic's. Though Simon had apprised her of their passenger's arrival, Brockmeyer had kept Jane so busy in the kitchen that she didn't get a glimpse of the sheik until it was time for her to go to the lounge to serve lunch.

She drew a deep breath before opening the door quietly and striding quickly across the lounge to the bar to choose the wine to accompany the meal. Kahlid and Dominic were sitting in the two large brown leather chairs in the center of the room, conversing lazily. Though Jake looked up when Jane came in the door, he didn't greet her, as he usually did, and she drew a breath of relief. It was clear that she was to be treated as just another steward, in the presence of Dominic's guest. She would have found it exceedingly uncomfortable to have to submit to Jake's teasing in front of this stranger.

Ahmet Kahlid's appearance was not exactly dashing, she noticed from the corner of her eye. His large, sturdy body was dressed in a gray business suit that screamed of Saville Row. He was well over six feet, with dark hair and beard and expressive dark eyes, which twinkled like bright buttons. He reminded her vaguely of a big, cozy teddy bear.

Jane pulled a bottle out of the wine rack and examined the label with satisfaction before placing it on the bar.

"No, not that one!" Jake called sharply, rising to his feet. "Excuse me, Ahmet, but there's a rather good wine I want you to try."

He strode across the room and behind the bar. Jane watched in surprise as he reached for a bottle of quite ordinary vintage. The one she had chosen was much better, she thought indignantly. She opened her lips to tell him this, then closed them quickly as she met Jake Dominic's dark, furious gaze.

"What the hell are you doing here?" he muttered in a harsh undertone. "I thought even Brockmeyer would have the sense to send a substitute, with Kahlid here."

"Why should he?" Jane hissed back indignantly. "I'm perfectly capable. Mr. Brockmeyer trusts me completely."

Jake Dominic muttered an imprecation beneath his breath and thrust the bottle at her. "I don't want to hear a word out of you, do you understand?" he asked, his eyes flashing. "And tell Brockmeyer I want a different steward by dinner."

He turned and walked back toward Kahlid, the smooth mask once more in place on his dark face. Jane stared after him, her face flushed with confusion and hurt at the sheer injustice of the attack. As she turned away, she intercepted Kahlid's curious, speculative gaze.

Jane was conscious of several such glances from Kahlid during lunch as she carefully obeyed Jake's orders. Not one word did she utter as she served each course and kept the wineglasses full. When not needed, she stood at rigid attention behind Jake Dominic's chair, her blazing golden eyes staring straight before her.

It was a building fury that caused her to make the blunder that was to have such far-reaching consequences. Her hand was shaking slightly as she refilled Kahlid's glass for the third time, and she splashed a little on the white damask tablecloth.

Without thinking she murmured absently in Arabic, "Forgive me, effendi," and dabbed at the spreading stain with a linen napkin.

Kahlid broke off what he was saying to Dominic to stare in surprise at Jane. "But this is a wonderful surprise, Jake. Why did you not tell me your little servant spoke Arabic?"

Dominic shot her a furious look before smiling coolly at Kahlid. "I have to confess to ignorance, Ahmet. I wasn't aware that she did."

Kahlid smiled gently at Jane and said in Arabic. "It warms my heart to hear my language on your lips, little one." He sighed mournfully, reminding her once more of a cuddlesome teddy bear. "One gets homesick for the sound of one's own tongue."

Jane's golden eyes were glowing with sympathy at his words. The sheik was really quite nice, she thought warmly. She, too, knew the longing to hear one's own language in a foreign land.

"I spent two years in Kuwait as a young child," she replied gently in Arabic. "I am pleased that my small accomplishment brings you pleasure."

"You may go, Jane," Dominic interrupted abruptly. "Please give Mr. Brockmeyer our compliments."

"No! No!" Kahlid protested, his shining eyes running eagerly over her, from the bright red curls to the tip of her sensible brown leather shoes. "Do not send her away, my friend. It pleases me to have her here. She is a most unusual type, *n'est-ce pas?*"

"Oh, most unusual," Jake answered dryly. "You might say she's one of a kind." His hand tightened imperceptibly on the stem of his wineglass as he gazed expressionlessly at Jane. "However, the girl has duties to perform in the kitchen. I'm afraid that you'll have to do without her."

"The kitchen!" Kahlid scoffed. "It is criminal to send this one to the kitchen, when she could give such pleasure to me. You have any number of servants who can work in the kitchen. Send one of them!" He turned to his friend with the pleading look of a lonesome puppy. "Assign this little Jane to me as my personal steward," he asked impulsively.

Jane's eyes widened in surprise as they flew to Jake's impassive face.

"Impossible," he said coolly. "As I said, Jane has other duties. I assure you that you'll be quite content with the steward whom Captain Benjamin has assigned you."

Kahlid shook his head stubbornly. "Content, perhaps, but not happy," he argued, his eyes running almost caressingly over Jane's heart-shaped face. "I know this little Jane could make me very happy," he finished softly.

A flicker of annoyance passed over Jake's face at Kahlid's persistence, but his tone was still even. "I said no, Ahmet."

It appeared that Kahlid was a man who did not recognize the meaning of the word. He smiled jovially.

"Then you must change your mind, my friend," he said persuasively. "You are not usually so inhospitable to your guests. What I have asked is not unreasonable. Did I not provide you with all that you could desire when you visited my home in Algiers last year?"

"You don't understand," Dominic said deliberately, "Jane is *my personal* servant."

The jovial smile faded from Kahlid's face, and he sighed despondently. "I suppose that I should have suspected. Never before have you had a female servant on your yacht." He turned back to Jane, his bright eyes regretful. "It is really too bad, little Jane; you would have brought me much pleasure." Without waiting for a reply from the bewildered girl, he asked Jake, "If you grow weary, you will send her to me?"

Dominic smiled mockingly. "Are you not my friend?" he asked evasively. He rose and threw his napkin on the table. "Now, if you will excuse me, I'd like a word with Jane before she returns to her duties. I'll join you in a moment."

He took Jane by the wrist and strode toward the door, forcing her almost to run to keep up with him. He did not stop until they were out of the room and on deck. When they'd reached a deserted area a little distance from the lounge, he released her wrist, but only to take her by the shoulders and swing her roughly around to face him.

His black eyes were blazing. "Was it too quiet for you?" he raged. "Was everything going so smoothly that you were compelled to raise a little hell just to make things interesting?"

"It's you who's raising a fuss over nothing," she said indignantly, trying futilely to pry those iron hands from her shoulders. "All I was trying to do was perform my duties as efficiently as I was able, and all you can do is yell at me and order me around. I didn't want to be there, you know!"

"It wasn't enough for you to come prancing into the lounge wriggling that cute little bottom in front of Kahlid, but you had to coo sweet nothings in Arabic to him," Jake said furiously. "Have you no sense at all?"

"Prance? Wriggle?" she squeaked, outraged. "I do not wriggle, and I was merely being courteous to the man. What was I supposed to do, ignore it when I spilled the wine?"

"You were supposed to serve lunch, keep your mouth shut, and stay the hell out of Kahlid's way. Now look what you've done, with all that melting tenderness and cooing."

Cooing? It was the second time he had used that nauseating word. "I do not coo," she said between her teeth. "I was merely being sympathetic to the poor man. He was obviously homesick and a little lonely. What harm did it do to show a little concern and kindness? I only uttered a few words to your friend."

"They were evidently the wrong words," Dominic snapped. "Ahmet was most persistent about having you assigned to him. What would you have done if I'd let him have you?"

"It wouldn't have been so bad for a few days," she said defiantly. "The poor man just wanted to have someone to talk to."

He shook her again, his face dark with exasperation. "Don't you realize that you'd have been in Ahmet's bed tonight if I hadn't refused to hand you over to him?"

Her golden eyes were astonished, and her mouth dropped open. "That's crazy," Jane said faintly, when she could speak. "He couldn't have meant that when he asked for me. He wouldn't have assumed that you could snap your fingers and order me into someone's bed just because I happen to work for you. This is the twentieth century!"

"Not in Kahlid's country," Jake replied grimly. "It's a different culture and a different century. Oh, he's got a surface sophistication, thanks to his Western education, but the basic beliefs are still very much alive in him. Did you know that he had two wives, last time I counted?"

That cozy teddy bear of a man? She had known from her stay in Kuwait that such arrangements existed in the East, but it appeared slightly incongruous in connection with Kahlid.

Dominic continued relentlessly. "It might interest you to know that he also keeps three or four pretty female servants at his home in Algiers in case his male guests want a woman."

"Is that what he meant when he said he provided you. . ." Jane's voice faltered.

"Why not?" he said, his voice hard. "As I said, it's a different culture. The women are more than willing, and they're free to leave Ahmet's house at any time." His dark eyes flickered. "I doubt if you would have proven so compliant."

Jane shook her head dazedly. "I still don't believe it," she protested. "I don't even have the looks Arabs admire. I'm much too thin."

"Kahlid has developed a variety of sexual appetites," Jake said meaningfully. "Believe me, you'd appeal to quite a few of them."

Her face was puzzled. "I don't understand."

"Forget it!" he snapped impatiently. "Just accept the fact that we have a problem, thanks to your blasted naïveté."

"But there's no problem now," she protested. "He accepted it very well when you convinced him you really meant your refusal."

"Heaven help me!" Jake swore. "He accepted it because I told him you were my personal servant. In other words, I've reserved you exclusively for my own bed."

Jane's face was now as scarlet as her hair. "Surely that wasn't necessary." She choked, her eyes not meeting his. "I could have just told him no. He seemed an understanding man when I spoke to him in the lounge."

"Kahlid is charming as long as he gets his own way, but in case you haven't noticed, he doesn't know how to accept a refusal. He just keeps plowing ahead like a bulldozer. Ahmet informs me he'll be with us at least until we reach Cozumel, and I assure you he'd be after you a large portion of that time. I have no desire to set a guard outside your door. Ahmet would consider it an insult."

"And I suppose that would be simply terrible," Jane said ironically. "We mustn't offend the man just because he may have the intention of raping me."

He shot her a quelling look. "As I've already explained to you, he wouldn't look at it the same way another man would. He would think your refusal was merely to tease him." He frowned. "I have no intention of antagonizing Kahlid if I can help it. He has enormous influence, and he was very useful to me last year when I was filming in Tunis."

"Charming!" Jane replied caustically, "Perhaps you should hand me over to him. After all, one must maintain one's contacts."

"Be quiet," Jake gritted, his black eyes flashing. "You've caused enough of a problem without adding your damn insolence to it." His lips thinned as he said ruthlessly, "I warned you I like things my own way, and that's exactly how I'm going to have it. I'm going to keep Kahlid resigned to the situation and moderately content. I'm going to keep my Middle East contact"—his eyes flickered cynically—"and if we're extremely lucky, I may keep you out of Kahlid's bed until he leaves the ship at Cozumel."

"And how do you intend to accomplish all this?" Jane challenged. "Move me into your bed instead?"

"That won't be necessary," Jake retorted coolly. "Ahmet won't expect you to sleep with me permanently or move into my cabin. That privilege is reserved for a mistress. A woman of your status would receive only an occasional invitation and a moderate amount of personal attention. Most of the time he would expect you to be treated exactly like any other servant."

"Then it will be quite easy to deceive him," Jane

said, relieved. "We need only continue as we are now."

"Not entirely," Jake said dryly. "Kahlid is no fool. We must spend some time alone together to give an appearance of intimacy." His eyes narrowed thoughtfully. "I think perhaps you'd better meet me each morning for a swim and have breakfast with me on deck. That should be adequate."

"Are you sure this is really necessary?" Jane asked unhappily, biting her lip. "You know what the crew is going to think if you start paying attention to me."

"Exactly what Kahlid is going to think," Jake said indifferently, then his eyes hardened. "Who are you worried about, the crew or Simon?" he asked harshly. "Do you think it will turn him off to think he may be sharing you with me?"

There was a look of shock and hurt on Jane's face, and quick tears filled her eyes. "There's nothing like that between Simon and me," she said huskily. "We're just good friends."

"Just good friends," Jake echoed. "Then you won't mind if he thinks what the rest do about you."

"I mind very much what he thinks about me," she said quietly. "I wouldn't want anyone to believe I was anything more than a member of the crew. It will be very painful and embarrassing to know that they think I'm just another one of your playmates."

For a moment there was a curious flicker of regret in Jake Dominic's eyes. "You should have thought of that before you involved us both in a situation that presents no other solution," he said curtly. "I can't get you out of *this* mess just by knocking a few heads together, Jane."

"I suppose not." She sighed despondently. "I just wish—"

"Too late for that," he interrupted tersely. "Meet me on deck at seven tomorrow morning and we'll begin our little charade." He dropped his hands from her shoulders and stepped back. "I rather expect your attitude should be respectfully adoring in public," he continued mockingly. "Work on it, will you?"

"I'll try," she said wryly. "You may have to use all your directorial skill to wring a plausible performance from me. I'm no actress."

"I'm fully aware of that," Jake said resignedly. "Why do you think I picked early morning for our supposed romantic trysts? Ahmet will be up and about only occasionally, and it shouldn't be too much of a strain on that blasted transparency of yours."

"Shall I tell Mr. Brockmeyer that I'm to be replaced as your meal steward?" Jane asked.

He shook his head. "Kahlid will expect you to continue, under the circumstances. In my place he would display you with a certain discreet pride of possession."

"You seem to understand him very well," Jane said slowly.

"Perhaps I do," he said cynically. "Kahlid and I aren't so very far apart in our rather primitive reactions to certain situations. You'd be wise to remember that."

Jane's eyes were troubled as she asked hesitantly, "Is there no other way? Couldn't you just release me from our agreement and send me home? I promise that I'd send you payments every month until the panel was paid for."

Jake's dark eyes sparked dangerously. "No, damn it, you stay here!" he said harshly, his face suddenly satanic in intensity. "You belong to me for the rest of the cruise. We'll handle the problem exactly as I've indicated."

Before she could answer, he had turned and walked away.

Seven

Jane should have guessed that any plan that Jake
Dominic had devised would be a total and unequivo-
cal success. The morning rendezvous obviously thoroughly convinced Kahlid of Jane's supposed position
in Dominic's life. After joining them two or three
times during the next week for breakfast and a swim,
Kahlid evidently decided his presence was an inva-
sion of their privacy and subsequently ordered breakfast in his cabin.

Though his absence relieved Jane from the strain
of acting the adoring paramour Jake had described,
their meetings were still charged with the same burning restlessness that had characterized their association before Kahlid's arrival.

Jane looked back wistfully at those first uncomplicated evenings they had spent in the lounge, bent in
amiable conflict over the chessboard. Now it seemed
that everything she said to Jake was wrong. She
seemed to have a talent for setting off that famous
mercurial temperament without the least effort,
and her own temper responded like a brushfire in a
strong wind.

She had reluctantly come to the conclusion that
Jake Dominic was entirely correct in his assessment

of Kahlid's attitude toward her and the necessity for
their charade. Though Ahmet was perfectly charming to her in their brief encounters when she acted
as steward, a few times she had noticed an apprais-
ing glance that was totally foreign to the innocent
teddy-bear image. Once, when he joined them for a
swim, his frank approval of her in the tiny bikini
verged on pure lechery.

It had struck her as positively ludicrous that a girl
of her quite ordinary appearance should provoke
passion in the breast of the sheik, and she had tried to
make Jake see how funny it was. She had finally
faltered and fallen silent before the stormy anger in
Jake's face. It appeared that she had blundered again,
she thought morosely. It seemed everything she did
these days was wrong.

During one of her periods of depression, she had
asked Jake if it might not be safe now to stop their
morning rendezvous, since Kahlid had ceased his
visits with them. The answer she received was rude,
explicit, and ended with Jake's telling her icily that
he would decide when they would call a halt to their
meetings, and would she please refrain from making
stupid suggestions.

After this savage, unprovoked attack she did,
indeed, refrain from making any suggestions at all,
as well as much conversation. Their time together,
before she could escape to the less demanding duties required by Brockmeyer, rapidly became a painful chore.

Jane had even taken to arriving on deck a few
minutes early and diving into the sea before Jake
Dominic arrived, so that she could have a few minutes by herself in the silken serenity of the cobalt
water. She desperately needed that time alone before
she faced the tension that his presence aroused.

Marc Benjamin was at the rail, staring absently at
the swimmer whose slick red head bobbed in and
out of the waves as she cleaved through the water
with smooth, economical strokes, when Jake Dominic appeared on deck one morning. The captain had

formed the habit of occasionally dropping by to have a cup of coffee and chat with the two of them before he went about his duties. He turned at the sound of the other man's footsteps and appraised the bronze, muscular figure in black swim trunks, a white terry-cloth robe slung carelessly over one shoulder. Marc Benjamin's calm eyes drifted up to Dominic's face, and he saw there the tense, restless frown he wore constantly of late.

"She's really very good," Benjamin commented casually, nodding toward the figure in the water.

Jake gave Jane a cursory glance before throwing his robe on the deck chair and turning to the captain. "A veritable water baby," he said caustically. "She tells me she learned to swim in Tahiti. One wonders how the island survived."

Ignoring the sarcasm, Benjamin continued to stare at Jane's distant figure. "It's strange that a girl who has knocked around the world as much as she has still retains that almost crystal simplicity."

Dominic did not reply, but his dark eyes turned to gaze at Jane's red, seallike head, his face taut. Benjamin glanced keenly at that face before asking softly, "Why don't you let her go, Jake? You're making her miserable."

Dominic's head jerked around, his eyes blazing. "Mind your own business, Marc. I won't tolerate your interference in this."

"She's just a kid. She doesn't understand," Benjamin continued calmly. "You've been ripping at her like a wounded tiger, and she doesn't know why."

Jake's mouth twisted. "And you think you do know?"

"I've known you for twelve years," Benjamin replied with a shrug. "I can make a pretty good guess about what's bothering you. Since you're not going to do anything about it, it's rather masochistic to keep her around, don't you think?"

Jake's eyes took on their familiar, shuttered look. "How do you know I have no intention of doing anything about it?" he said obliquely. "Perhaps I'm just biding my time."

Benjamin shook his head. "You haven't the patience for that type of cat-and-mouse game. Let her go, Jake. You can't claim that she amuses you now."

Dominic laughed harshly. "No, by God, I can't claim that. But I'm not letting her go." His hand tightened on the rail. "Stay out of it, Marc."

Benjamin sighed and turned back to watch Jane's bikini-clad figure, now floating lazily on its back. "Well, I tried," he said philosophically. "She deserved that from me."

Jake Dominic turned moodily to follow his gaze, and suddenly his body stiffened. "Oh, my God!" he breathed, his face turning white.

Benjamin's keen eyes roamed the horizon searchingly, and then he too froze in horror. Not a hundred yards from that small, unaware figure was a triangular gray fin, lazily cleaving the water.

"We've got to warn her!" the captain said, and raised his hands to his mouth to make his shout more resonant.

"No!" Jake grabbed his friend's arm. "Don't startle her. I don't think he's seen her yet. She's safer if she makes no motion to attract his attention. Get two life preservers ready." He poised to dive at the open rail.

"Jake! For God's sake let me shout and warn her!" Marc urged. "What's the sense of your both being in danger?"

Jake ignored him and dived cleanly into the sea.

Jane could feel the warm sun on her wet face and see bits of blue sky through her half-closed lids as she let the sea cradle her floating body with its gentle rocking motion. It was divinely peaceful just to give yourself up to the elements and let them take you where they would, like a bit of flotsam, she thought dreamily. In the vastness of the great soothing sea, even the roar of Brockmeyer or the biting sarcasm of Jake Dominic seemed unimportant and far away.

The Publisher of Loveswept® Romances invites you to:

CLAIM A FREE EXCLUSIVE ROMANCE

Lift Here

...PLUS SIX ROMANCES RISK FREE

6 ROMANCES FREE

Detach and affix this stamp to the postage-paid reply card and mail at once!

NO OBLIGATION TO BUY!

THE FREE GIFT IS YOURS TO KEEP

SEE DETAILS INSIDE ▶

LET YOURSELF BE LOVESWEPT BY... SIX BRAND NEW LOVESWEPT ROMANCES!

Because Loveswept romances sell themselves ...we want to send you six (Yes, six!) exciting new novels to enjoy for 15 days — risk free! — without obligation to buy

Discover how these compelling stories of contemporary romances tug at your heart strings and keep you turning the pages. Meet true-to-life characters you'll fall in love with as their romances blossom. Experience their challenges and triumphs — their laughter, tears and passion.

Let yourself be Loveswept! Join our **at-home reader service!** Each month we'll send you six new Loveswept novels **before they appear in the bookstores.** Take up to **15 days to preview** current selections **risk-free! Keep only those shipments you want.** Each book is yours for only $2.09 plus postage & handling, and sales tax where applicable — **a savings of 41¢ per book** off the cover price.

NO OBLIGATION TO BUY — WITH THIS RISK-FREE OFFER!

YOU GET SIX
ROMANCES RISK FREE...
Plus AN EXCLUSIVE TITLE FREE!

Loveswept Romances

```
AFFIX
RISK FREE
BOOKS
STAMP
HERE.
```

Kay Hooper's
Larger Than Life

This FREE gift
is yours to keep.

MY "NO RISK" GUARANTEE

There's no obligation to buy and the free gift is mine to keep. I may preview each subsequent shipment for 15 days. If I don't want it, I simply return the books within 15 days and owe nothing. If I keep them, I will pay just $2.09 per book. I save $2.50 off the retail price for the 6 books (plus postage and handling, and sales tax where applicable).

YES! Please send my six Loveswept novels
RISK FREE along with my FREE GIFT
described inside the heart!   **BR987**   10124

NAME_____

ADDRESS_____APT_____

CITY_____

STATE_____ZIP_____

DETACH AND MAIL CARD TODAY

FREE BOOK OFFER!

PREVIEW SIX BRAND-NEW
LOVESWEPT ROMANCES RISK FREE
...PLUS A FREE EXCLUSIVE ROMANCE

NO PURCHASE REQUIRED
THE FREE GIFT IS YOURS TO KEEP

BUSINESS REPLY MAIL
FIRST-CLASS MAIL   PERMIT NO. 2456   HICKSVILLE, NY

POSTAGE WILL BE PAID BY ADDRESSEE

Loveswept

Bantam Books
P.O. Box 985
Hicksville, NY 11802-9827

NO POSTAGE
NECESSARY
IF MAILED
IN THE
UNITED STATES

"Stay exactly as you are," Jake's voice ordered crisply. "Be very still and just listen to me."

Her eyes opened to see Jake's white, taut face above her, his dark eyes sharp. Oh, Lord, she thought unhappily, he was in his usual black mood. She instinctively started to swing her body upright, when he grabbed her by the chin and said, "Damn it, be still! I should have known you couldn't take a single order without messing it up."

She looked up to reply indignantly, when she noticed he wasn't looking at her at all but at something over her head, and that his bronze face was a shade paler than usual. "What is it?" she asked quietly, not moving.

He looked down at her, his dark eyes flickering, an exhilarated smile on his face, "We're going to play lifesaver," he said lightly. "You're going to be the victim and I'm the rescuer, and I don't want you to move a muscle. Understand?"

"I understand," she whispered, and turned her head slowly to where he had been gazing a few seconds ago.

"Oh, no!" Her cry was almost a whimper as she glimpsed that menacing fin. A surge of primal terror shot through her.

"Don't panic," he ordered quickly, starting to propel her through the water with a smooth, easy crawl. "He hasn't spotted us yet, and we just might get back to the ship before he does. The important thing to remember is not to make any wild splashing movements or rhythmic sounds. Either one will attract a shark's notice."

She smiled through teeth that had a tendency to chatter with terror. "You mean like the noise a swimmer would make as he splashed through the water?" she asked throatily. It seemed insane for them to be moving and talking so calmly, when close by a hungry monster with sharp teeth was searching the blue waters for his breakfast.

"Exactly!" Jake said with a trace of his mocking grin. "That's why you're playing victim. It lessens both the motion and the noise factor for me to do all the work." He looked over his shoulder. "We're almost halfway to the ship. We may make it yet." Dominic looked down into her strained face, and she was again conscious of the strange ghost of excitement deep in those dark eyes. "Marc will throw us two life preservers when we get within reach of the ship. Grab one, put it on, and hold on for dear life." He actually laughed at the irony of the unintentional pun. What kind of a man was he that he could laugh at a time like this, she wondered dazedly.

"Marc and some of the men will jerk you out of the water and onto the deck. We're almost two-thirds of the way home," he commented with another look over his shoulder. "If I tell you to swim for it, I want you to swim like blazes for the ship, but quietly, with a minimum of splashing. Okay?"

"Okay," she choked out, wondering what difference it would make at that terrifying point how much splashing she made.

But he didn't have to tell her, as it happened. Marc Benjamin's voice came over the water in a clarion call. "He's seen you! God! Hurry, damn it!"

"Go!" Jake ordered curtly, turning her over with lightning swiftness and giving her a mighty starting shove through the water.

Jane's arms moved under the water with a panic-driven urgency that propelled her through the water like a small torpedo. She could dimly hear Jake to the right of her and remembered with relief that he was an even stronger swimmer than she was. He would make the ship in a few more swift strokes.

She lifted her head, and there was the *Sea Breeze* before her, white and beautiful in the morning sunlight, with Marc Benjamin and several seamen standing tense and still at the rail. A life preserver floated a few feet in front of her, and she slipped it over her head and under her armpits.

"My God, pull her up! He's right behind her!" Benjamin's voice contained a chilling panic, and Jane could feel her breath stop in her lungs. There was a tremendous splashing in back of her. Was he so close, then? she thought. Was she to be ravaged by those razor-sharp teeth when she was within seconds of being rescued?

Then she was jerked out of the water with a mighty heave. She dangled awkwardly for a few seconds and then was pulled the rest of the way up to the deck. Several pairs of eager hands reached out to receive her, and she collapsed on the deck, her breast heaving with exertion and fear. A towel was thrown around her shaking shoulders, and she sat up, looking around quickly for Jake. He wasn't there!

Jane noticed for the first time that the captain and the men were still at the rail, the silence gripping them ominously tense. No, he couldn't still be in the water with that gray horror! Why hadn't they pulled him out? She was on her feet, elbowing her way through the men at the rail. She stared down at the water that had cradled her so lovingly such a short time ago and now seemed to hold all the horrors of hell. There was Jake's crisp black head, but he seemed so terribly far away from the white life-preserver in the water.

"He was right beside me," she whispered to Benjamin, her hand grabbing his arm in a panicky grip. "My God, what happened? He was right beside me!"

His eyes did not leave the triangular gray fin that seemed to be circling behind Dominic's powerful, still-moving figure. "The shark was headed right for you," he said tersely. "We would never have gotten you out in time. Jake cut through the water between you to divert him."

That loud splashing, she thought dazedly, it had been Jake, deliberately baiting the shark away from her.

"He's going to die," she moaned, as she watched the strong arms cleave through the water with boundless vitality. "He's going to die, and it's all my fault."

"No, I think he's going to make it." Benjamin's voice was tense. "His actions seemed to have confused the shark. He's been circling like that since we pulled you on board."

"Oh, God, please," she prayed, her eyes on that swimming figure that suddenly, wonderfully, seemed closer. "Please let him live. Please let him be all right."

Then the life preserver was over Jake's head and under his armpits. With a motion from the captain, he was jerked out of the water in the same graceless fashion that Jane had been. A cheer went up from the men as, hand over hand, they pulled him aboard like a fresh-caught marlin. They crowded around him, ridding him of the life preserver and slapping him on the back in congratulations, laughing and jesting in the sudden relief from tension.

Jane sank down on the deck, her legs suddenly too weak to hold her. She leaned against the rail, forgotten for the moment while the crew gathered around Jake. She was content to have it so. She only wanted to sit there and run her eyes over the vibrant aliveness that was Jake Dominic. It seemed a miracle that he should be there, sitting on the deck, the white towel draped over his bronze shoulders, his eyes gleaming with that familiar mocking deviltry that she had thought might be extinguished forever.

Jane felt that she was opening up like a flower as she sat looking at that dark face. The petals of her soul were blossoming and reaching forth to a sudden maturity that was as irreversible as it was beautiful. She knew with almost painful clarity that she loved Jake Dominic and would until the day she died. It was a fact so simple and undeniable that she had no defense against it. How many times had she pushed that knowledge away, afraid to admit to herself that no one else could cause her the joy and pain that he could with a word or a twitch of that crooked eyebrow? Not until that terrible moment when she thought she might lose him had the truth burst on her with the force of an exploding nova. She didn't want to live in a world without Jake Dominic. She'd want to die also if that vibrant, complex man was taken from her.

She closed her eyes. Oh, God, for once, couldn't she have done something with less than her usual all-or-nothing style? He filled her whole life, making everything else seem unimportant in comparison.

She opened her eyes as she heard Benjamin's teasing voice across the deck. "Jake, you looked like a bloody bullfighter, cutting across in front of Jane like that. I was wishing I had a cape to throw you."

Jake Dominic pulled a face, then stood up and began to dry his hair with the towel that had been draped around his shoulders. "I would have appreciated a speargun more," he said dryly, his black eyes dancing.

Suddenly the captain reached back and touched a red stain on the white towel. "This is blood!" he said sharply. "Where are you hurt, Jake?"

Jane sat up as alert as if she'd been galvanized. Oh, no, let him not be hurt, she thought feverishly, not now!

Jake grinned lazily. "It's just a graze on my back—the shark caught me with a tooth as I swam past."

Benjamin was behind him looking at the wound with critical eyes. "It's not too bad," he decided. "But I'd better put something on it. It's a good thing it didn't bleed more; it would have driven the shark into a frenzy."

Jane could feel the blood draining from her face at the casual remark, and she pulled herself to her feet, clinging desperately to the rail. Jake had been so close to death, down there in the water. If the cut had been deeper . . . if the shark hadn't been confused . . . So close.

She saw with unbelieving eyes that both Jake and Marc were chuckling as if nothing had happened. Then she suddenly remembered Jake Dominic's expression as he pulled her along behind him—that flicker of excitement deep in the mocking eyes. He had even laughed, she thought incredulously. He had gotten some sort of queer kick out of playing with death. He had almost died, his life had almost ended, and he had laughed! She felt a burning anger start deep inside her. It was her life too that he was risking so carelessly—she wouldn't have wanted to live without him.

She moved forward slowly, pushing through the crowd that surrounded Jake Dominic, her legs shaking with a strange fatigue but charged with the force of her fury.

The laughter died in Jake's dark eyes as he caught sight of Jane's white face and blazing gold stare. His keen glance swiftly took in the violent trembling that was causing her limbs to shake, and there was a flash of concern in his face.

She stopped a few paces from the two men, her eyes fixed desperately on Jake's face. "You enjoyed it!" she accused hoarsely. "Damn you! You enjoyed it!"

Jake moved forward impulsively. "Jane—"

"You laughed!" she cried, the tears running down her face. "You got some kind of wild kick out of it all." Suddenly her fists started beating wildly at his bare, hair-roughened chest. "Damn you! Damn you!" The tears poured down her cheeks and great sobs shook her body, as her legs suddenly gave way and she felt herself falling.

Jake caught her and swung her up in his arms in one swift movement. She dimly heard Benjamin murmur, "Shock," as she clung desperately to Dominic's broad shoulders and buried her head in the wiry dark hair on his chest, while the sobs continued to rack her body.

"I'll take her," Benjamin offered quietly, and he took a step closer. Jane felt Jake's arms tighten around her, and she clung even more desperately at the threat of being separated from that vibrant strength that was now the center of her universe.

"No!" he said. "I'll take her to her cabin. Fetch her some hot tea with plenty of sugar," he said over his shoulder. "Maybe a sedative, too."

Jane could not seem to stop her tears as Dominic

carried her swiftly to her cabin and deposited her on the narrow single bed. He would have withdrawn his arms and stepped back, but she held onto him in a stranglehold, still sobbing piteously.

"Jane!" Dominic said with exasperation, trying to pry her arms from around his neck. "Jane, damn it, let me go! I've got to get this wet suit off of you."

She barely heard him, but he finally managed to unclamp her clinging arms. He sat down beside her on the bed and with swift, experienced hands stripped the wet bikini off her shaking body and wrapped her, like a papoose-child, in the warm gold blanket that he found at the foot of the bed. He went into the bathroom and came out with a thick white towel and proceeded to dry her hair, with more vigor than gentleness.

The sobs were subsiding now, but the tears still poured from a seemingly inexhaustible fount while she watched him with feverishly intent eyes. He cared for her as gently as if she were a beloved child. His face was set and stern, his dark mocking eyes strangely serious. When he'd finished these tasks, he threw the towel on the floor beside the bed and merely sat looking at her, his eyes filled with a helpless exasperation at the tears that wouldn't cease.

"Damn it, Jane, you'll make yourself sick," he said huskily. "Stop it!"

"Hold me," she whispered. "Just hold me, please." She fought to release her arms from the strictures of the gold blanket to pull him to her, but he stopped her with a swift movement.

"No, lie still, I'll come to you."

He stretched full length on the narrow bed beside her and pulled her blanket-wrapped body into his arms, fitting her head in the curve of his shoulder. "Now, will you stop that damn crying?" he said hoarsely, his hands running soothingly over her back through the wool blanket.

She knew a dreamy contentment as he continued to stroke and caress her while she lay curled against him. She even imagined she felt a light kiss pressed against her temple when she snuggled to get even closer to him.

"I can come back later," Benjamin said dryly from the door.

Jake muttered an imprecation and jerked away from Jane as if he'd been burned. "She's shaking," he said, running his hand through his hair as he swung off the bed and onto his feet. "And she can't stop crying."

"May I suggest that a heating pad and a large handkerchief might prove to be considerably safer for the girl?" Marc offered politely, coming forward with a glass of water and two tablets in his hands.

Jake shot him a quelling glance and took the water and tablets. He sat back down on the bed and cradled Jane's shoulders in one arm while he fed her the pills and water. She took them like an obedient child, and as he laid her carefully back on the pillow he observed with anxiety the dark circles beneath her eyes and the pale, pinched cheeks. "She's too damn docile," he said thickly. "Where's the tea?"

"She won't need it," Benjamin answered laconically. "She'll be out in a few minutes. That sedative is fairly strong."

Already Jane could feel the fuzziness that dulled the edges of their voices above her head and lessened the nameless urgency that drove her to keep Jake within constant reach of her hand. She could see Marc Benjamin's speculative gray gaze as if from far away.

"You know, I would never have thought that she would fall apart like this," she heard the captain say thoughtfully. "She's really a very strong personality."

Jake turned on him savagely. "She was almost eaten alive by a shark!" he said explosively. "How the hell do you expect her to react?"

Benjamin shook his head. "Take it easy. I'm not impugning the courage of your little lamb," he drawled. "We both know that she's got plenty of it. It was just a comment." He moved forward to put a hand on Jake's shoulder. "You'd better come along and let me tend to that graze."

"In a minute," Jake said absently, putting the glass on the bedside table and brushing the red ringlets away from Jane's forehead. "I don't want to leave her like this."

She could dimly see his concerned face hovering over her, before her lids closed unexpectedly and there was only the darkness.

Jane awoke several times that day, only to fall back into that cocoon of sleep. She was conscious of Jake's presence several times, and of the sound of voices reverberating as if from the bottom of a well, but she could make no sense of the words. Once Simon was there with a luncheon tray, a worried expression on his handsome young face, but she couldn't rouse herself from her lethargy enough to obey his plea to eat something. She only wanted to return to the healing darkness.

It was late afternoon when the sedative finally wore off. She was alone in the cabin when she opened her eyes and looked around sluggishly. Her mouth felt dry and sour, she had a dull, throbbing ache in her head. That sedative must have had the force of a blackjack, she thought blearily, as she struggled to her feet on legs made of rubber. She dropped the gold blanket on the bed and then snatched it up again as she remembered that she was naked and her tiny cabin had recently resembled a Cecil B. De Mille crowd scene.

She vaguely remembered Jake's removing her tiny bikini, but she felt no embarrassment at the thought. Holding the blanket around her, she stumbled to the chest of drawers and drew out the gauzy green polka-dot shorty pajamas. She put them on hurriedly and ducked into the bath to brush her teeth and wash her face.

She was feeling ridiculously weak as she tottered back to the bed and slipped between the sheets. On the bedside table she discovered a thermos of rich beef broth, but she had only a scant cup before she was overcome with the lethargy that she seemed unable to conquer. She barely managed to pull the cover up about her before she was asleep once again.

Probably because the principal effect of the drug had worn off, her sleep was much lighter and more restless. She was plagued by hideous nightmares in which she was being chased by a giant shark with horrible sharp teeth, and each time she was about to be savaged, Jake Dominic swam in front of the monster and was devoured in her place.

Over and over the dream replayed in her subconscious, until she awoke with a shrill scream of pure agony on her lips.

Jake's face was above her, his face drawn with anxiety. He was shaking her roughly. "Damn it, wake up," he said harshly. "For God's sake, it's only a dream. Come out of it, baby!"

She threw herself at him, wrapping her arms around him convulsively while the silent tears flowed down her face. "You're alive!" she whispered achingly, her ear pressed to his chest. She could feel the steady throbbing of his heart through the fine material of his shirt, and it was gloriously reassuring. "I thought you were dead. I thought he'd eaten you!"

"I'm fine. It's you we've been worried about." He pushed her away to look at her face. His hand brushed at her tear-stained cheek with a gesture of exasperation. "If you don't stop that crying, you'll drown us both."

Jane chuckled huskily and wiped her eyes childishly with the back of her hand. "I'm sorry. I can't seem to stop. Stupid, isn't it?"

"Very," he said succinctly, as he pulled a handkerchief from his pocket and handed it to her. "Just the sort of thing that I would expect from an annoying brat like you."

She smiled, thinking how handsome he looked in his navy-blue slacks and white sport coat.

"I'm all right now," she assured him, wiping her eyes thoroughly. "I expect it was only the nightmare. Please go on to dinner."

"My dear girl, dinner was three hours ago. I was just stopping by to check on you before I called it a night." A startled glance at the bedside clock verified that it was after eleven. She had slept all day and half the evening! "Ahmet sends his regards and hopes that you'll be well enough to receive a call from him tomorrow."

"Oh, I'll be back to work tomorrow," Jane said, surprised. "I'm fine now."

"So fine that you wake up screaming," Jake said grimly, his eyes fixed on the delicacy of her heart-shaped face. "We'll see how you are in the morning."

"It was only the nightmares," she insisted, her eyes darkening with strain. "I keep having the same dream over and over." She shivered uncontrollably.

"I can guess what about," he said slowly. "An experience like that may give you nightmares for some time to come."

Jane swallowed anxiously at the thought of facing that horror every time she fell asleep. "I suppose so," she replied nervously, moistening her lips. "Well, I'll just have to contend with them, won't I?" She smiled shakily.

"The hell you will!" Jake said abruptly, his dark eyes flaming. "I'm not about to let you shake yourself to pieces in this clothes closet of a cabin."

"It's quite a nice cabin," she said defensively, looking up at him in bewilderment.

"Jane, for God's sake, don't argue with me. I do not intend to spend the rest of the night in this cracker box holding your hand, after already spending the best part of the day here. There's just not enough room!" He stooped and picked her up in his arms, blanket and all, and strode swiftly from the cabin.

She looked up into his grim face and asked quietly. "I hate to be overly curious, but may I ask where you're taking me?"

"Why, to my bed, of course." She stiffened in surprise, and he mistook her response for resistance. "Don't fight me, Jane. I'm not leaving you alone tonight. You can battle your own dragons some other night, when you're more fit." His mouth twisted cynically. "You can't claim that one night in my bed will ruin your reputation, when everyone on the ship assumes you're already very familiar with it."

When she merely continued to look at him with wide eyes, he went on aggressively. "Damn it, I'm not about to rape you, redhead, I just want to take care of you." His mouth twisted wryly, as he added, "In a bed where I won't develop a displaced sacroiliac."

She didn't answer, but her arms tightened around him nervously as he opened the door to his cabin and marched across the room to the king-sized bed and deposited her on the black velvet spread. He stepped back to look down at her still figure with wary dark eyes.

"What, no arguments?" he asked, arching an eyebrow inquiringly. "I expected you to fight me tooth and nail. You must be in worse shape than I thought."

She looked up at him serenely, her hair a brilliant flame on the black spread. "Why should I fight you?" she asked quietly. "You're quite right. I don't have any reputation to lose and I don't want to be alone tonight."

The wariness was still in his eyes. "That's very sensible of you," he said skeptically. "Not at all what one would expect from a frightened virgin."

"Really?" Jane sat up and threw off the gold blanket. "I'll try to act more in character next time."

His dark eyes were fixed compulsively on the bodice of the shorty nightgown. Her high firm breasts were clearly outlined beneath the gauzy material, even to the shadowy pink of her nipples.

"Not on my account," he drawled softly as he came toward her. His hand reached out to stroke her cheek with a gentle hand. "You look like a baby fresh from its bath," he said lightly. His hand rubbed her cheekbone with the sensual pleasure of a man stroking his favorite kitten.

Her breath caught in her throat, and she looked up into his dark eyes and saw a flicker in the hidden depths that caused her heart to increase its tempo. Then the flicker was gone and he had turned and walked toward the bathroom.

The usual mockery was in his voice as he said over his shoulder. "If you want to spare me your girlish blushes, I'd turn out the light." He disappeared into the bathroom.

Jane dove into the black velvet bed as if a nude Jake Dominic were going to appear the next instant. Then she had to jump out again to flick out the light by the door, and scrambled back under the covers again. It seemed an incredibly short time until the light in the bathroom was off and the door opened. She stiffened involuntarily as the bed sank under Dominic's weight when he slipped beneath the covers. She could feel the mattress shift while he stretched out like a cat, then turned over to rest on his back.

There was a moment of strained silence that stretched on interminably before he suddenly spoke. "For God's sake, relax!" he said with exasperation. "I'm not going to pounce on you. I can feel you trembling clear over here."

"I'm sorry," she whispered shakily, "I guess I'm nervous. I've never done anything like this before."

"That makes two of us," he said wryly, turning his shadowy face to where she lay. "I think I can safely say that I've never occupied a bed with a woman without intending to reap the full benefit."

"It must be difficult for you," she said huskily. "I never meant to be such a bother."

"Be quiet," he said impatiently. "And for pity's sake stop that trembling."

There was a moment of tension that was as fine as a stretched violin string. "Jake." Her voice was a hesitant whisper. "Will you hold me?"

She heard him inhale sharply and felt the sudden tension that tautened his body. "You can't be that innocent," he said roughly. "Don't try to play games with me, Jane. I'm finding this situation difficult enough."

She too was finding it difficult enough, she thought

wildly. It had taken all her courage to voice that whispered plea, and she had only impressed him as being a tease. She took a deep breath, and before she could change her mind, she scooted over suddenly to press against the warmth of his naked body with trembling urgency.

"Please, Jake," she said huskily, pressing her soft lips to the throbbing pulse in his throat. "I'm not playing any games."

His body stiffened as if electrified, and his arms automatically went around her. "My God," he said raggedly. His arms tightened ruthlessly. "Damn it, how much do you think I can take?"

His hands began a feverish sensual symphony over her shoulders and back while his lips touched hotly on her ears and throat. Then his lips found hers, and it was like no kiss she had ever known. It was as if he were famished for the taste and texture of her. His mouth rubbed and caressed her own with frantic hunger before parting her lips to probe intimately with his tongue, and his hands moved down to cup her bottom and lift her to his aroused loins with heated urgency. His lips ravished her with breathless need while he rubbed her softness against his muscular body with frenzied movements.

He buried his lips in her throat, his voice muffled as he said hoarsely, "God, I want you! I've been going insane for weeks. Open your mouth, love, I want every bit of you." His lips covered hers again, and she felt as if she were writhing in a flame of need. She moaned deep in her throat, and he chuckled huskily. "What a lovely sound," he groaned, his chest heaving. "I'm going to enjoy making you cry out for me, sweetheart."

Her hands slipped around his neck to become entangled in the crisp darkness of his hair, while his hand slipped under the loose gauze top to cup her small breasts in his hands, his thumbs teasing the nipples while his tongue invaded her mouth in numerous maddening forays.

She arched against him helplessly and again made

a sound more purr than moan. "Jake, please, I want
. . ." She trailed off as he suddenly lifted the gauze
top to bare her breasts to his ravaging lips and
tongue.

He chuckled again. "I know what you want, little
love," he said mischievously, nibbling teasingly at a
rosy nipple. "And I have every intention of giving it
to you." His tongue toyed with the other peak lazily.
"In my own time. Damn, I knew you'd be this
responsive!"

He rolled her over and with deft experienced hands
pulled the gauze top over her head and threw it to
the side. "How lovely you are," he said thickly, as his
hands cupped her breasts. "All strength and silk
and fire." His head bent slowly to take her lips in a
long slow kiss. "I've got to have you, Jane," he said
hoarsely. "If you don't want it, for God's sake tell me
to stop." He nibbled at the lobe of her ear. "I'm going
to take you if you don't tell me no."

Her hands caressed the light stubble on his cheek
with loving hands. "I'll never tell you no, Jake
Dominic," she said tenderly, "until the day that you
tell me to leave you."

His body stiffened above her, and he was suddenly
still. His lips lingered for a moment on her earlobe,
and then he breathed incredulously. "My God, what
am I doing?"

In one swift movement he rolled away from her,
leaving her bewildered, and chilled without the
warmth of his arms. He reached over and fumbled
with the lamp on the bedside table. Suddenly the
cabin was illuminated by a pool of light.

Jane sat up dazedly, her golden eyes smoky and
clouded with desire, her bare breasts still swollen
and rosy from his lips. What had happened? she
wondered in bewilderment as she watched Jake swing
out of bed and march angrily to the wardrobe. When
he returned, he was shrugging into a wine velour
robe, and he tossed her a man's white shirt.

"Cover up!"

She looked up pleadingly into his dark eyes, but there was relentless purpose in their ebony depths. She slipped on the white shirt and began to button it despondently. "What did I do wrong?" she asked quietly.

"Not a damn thing," he said harshly, his black eyes flashing. "It was as pretty a seduction as I've ever seen. You had me crazy for you."

She brushed the flaming ringlets from her forehead, her puzzled eyes on his dark angry face. He fumbled in the drawer of the nightstand and drew out a pack of cigarettes and an ashtray, which he placed on the table.

"I didn't know you smoked," she said, rolling up the sleeves of the shirt.

"I don't. I gave it up years ago," he answered harshly as he lit one and inhaled deeply. "I keep them around for moments of stress, and this, my dear Jane, is definitely a moment of stress!" He sat down on the bed and eyed her bare golden legs impatiently. She quickly straightened and tucked them under her tailor fashion.

His face was set and hard, and he spoke curtly. "I'm in no mood for evasion, Jane, so you'd be wise to be honest with me. You knew exactly what you were doing to me tonight. You also knew that I had no intention of taking you, before you staged your seduction scene." His lips twisted sardonically. "May I ask why I was chosen to initiate you into the carnal arts? It couldn't be, by any chance, that you'd taken it into that tiny little mind that you owe me something?"

Her gold eyes widened. "Owe you something?" she asked, puzzled. It had never occurred to her that he would interpret her action as anything but what it was.

"It's remarkably coincidental that the day I'm instrumental in saving you from a shark, you feel called upon to present me with your nubile young body."

"It's true I owe you my life," she said quietly. "But that isn't the reason that I want to belong to you."

"Then may I ask why I'm so honored?" he asked, looking down at his cigarette with narrowed eyes.

"I love you," she said simply, her golden eyes serene.

His dark gaze flew to meet hers, and he smiled cynically. "I might be touched if I thought you knew what you were talking about. If such an emotion exists, it's not the hodgepodge of gratitude and sex that you're feeling right now."

"You're wrong, gratitude has nothing to do with it," she said softly, her eyes lingering on the bold planes of his face. "As for sex, if this sample was anything to go by, it promises to be pretty terrific, but I made the first move before I knew that, Jake."

His gaze returned to the glowing end of his cigarette. "So when did you get this great revelation?" he asked mockingly. "I saw no sign of it before tonight."

"I only knew today," she said calmly. "I watched you sitting on that deck looking so blasted pleased with yourself that I wanted to murder you, and I knew that I'd love you forever." Her lips twisted wryly. "It came as quite a shock to me."

"And you say it's not gratitude," he scoffed. "Let's face it, Jane, you were in a highly emotional state and you convinced yourself that you were feeling something that just wouldn't exist under normal conditions."

She shook her head, her lips curving in a tender smile. "If you want to believe that, I can't stop you. I just know what I feel, Jake."

His eyes were diamond-hard as he looked up again. "Then you'd better get over it damn quick. In case you hadn't noticed, I'm not a safe person to care about. You'd come out of any relationship with me covered with battle scars. I don't think you could survive the game the way I play it."

She smiled sadly. "Don't worry about me—I'll survive," she said gently. "You're not responsible in any way."

He muttered a curse beneath his breath and crushed the cigarette out in the ashtray. "Charming," he said savagely. "So I'm to take what you offer and when I tire of you, simply cast you aside?"

"I hope not," she replied tranquilly. "I'm going to work very hard to make sure that I always have a place in your life." Her expression was endearingly earnest as she continued. "I promise I won't make things uncomfortable for you."

"You're not going to get the chance," he said roughly. "I've never found the idea of seducing innocents particularly appealing, and I have no intention of assuming the responsibility of your brand of commitment." His lips tightened ruthlessly. "I admit that I have a yen for that alluring little body of yours, but I can satisfy that urge with any number of women." His eyes were merciless on her suddenly pale face. "Benjamin said I should have sent you home, and he was right. You leave tomorrow."

She had listened to him silently, pain gradually dulling the gold of her eyes. She shook her head. "I won't go," she told him quietly. "I won't be a bother to you, but I won't leave you either, Jake."

"God, what a little fool you are!" he said brutally. "Don't you know when you're fighting a losing cause? I use women, I don't love them. What makes you think that a fresh-faced college kid is going to change my mind?"

"I don't expect you to love me," she answered passionately. "I only know that I love you and want to be with you. I don't know what place I'll find in your life. But whether it's as your mistress or your friend or just a steward on the *Sea Breeze*, I won't stand any chance at all if I let you send me away. I'm not leaving you, Jake!"

"I think you will," he said coolly, "when you find what a mistake you're making."

She shook her head, her eyes bright with unshed tears. "I told you once that there is only one way for me. It's still the truth, Jake."

His dark eyes were burning fitfully as he stared into her woebegone face. "Damn it to hell." His tone was exasperated. "You know I'll hurt you if you stay. Why can't you be sensible and put a few thousand miles between us? You just might be safe then."

She shook her head again, and suddenly two tears brimmed over and ran silently down her cheeks.

"Oh God, not again!" he groaned, and pulled her into his arms, rocking her as if she were a child and pushing her face into the soft velour of his robe. He stroked her hair gently for a long peaceful moment before he pleaded huskily, "Won't you please go away, redhead? I don't want to hurt you."

Jane nestled closer to his strong, warm body, her hand tangled intimately in the wiry dark patch of hair on his chest. She pressed her lips lovingly to his shoulder. "I have a chance," she whispered. "You like me." She kissed him again. "You want me. That's quite a bit to start with."

His chuckle reverberated under her ear. "You're so blasted determined," he said softly, his fingers gently rubbing the sensitive cord behind her ear. "I'm going to get rid of you, you know. I won't stand by and watch you mess up your life for an infatuation."

"You can try to discourage me tomorrow," she whispered teasingly. "But will you hold me tonight?"

He laughed again and shook his head ruefully. "Not on your life, redhead," he told her firmly. "I'm not about to let you consolidate your position in that particular fashion. We both know that you'd be my mistress by morning."

"Exactly," she said, grinning.

He slapped her lightly on her bottom and then pushed her firmly away. Pulling back the covers, he motioned sternly. "Get in, brat, and stay on your own side from now on."

She scrambled happily under the covers and scooted obediently to the far side of the bed. Without removing his robe, he also slipped beneath the covers, and flipped out the lamp. Jane sighed with contentment as she curled up on her side and prepared to go to sleep, which she did in only a few minutes.

On the other side of the broad expanse of mattress, Jake Dominic listened to the girl's even breathing with a grim smile on his face and eyes that were alert and wide awake. It was several hours later before he too fell asleep.

Eight

Simon was waiting for her on deck a few mornings later, and, as he turned to watch her hurrying toward him, Jane felt a thrill of uneasiness as she noticed the troubled expression on his usually sunny face.

"What is it, Simon?" she asked, puzzled.

"Look, Jane, it's none of my business," he burst out abruptly, running a hand through his blond hair. "But I thought someone should tell you."

Jane felt a cold finger of fear run down her spine at Simon's words. Her mind jumped immediately to the subject that dominated her life these days. She turned away to stare sightlessly at the sparkling sapphire sea. If Jake insisted, how could she prevent him from physically ejecting her from the *Sea Breeze*? Was this why Simon was so embarrassed and hesitant this morning?

Simon drew a deep breath. "Jane, I don't know how deeply you're involved with Jake Dominic, and I won't ask you to confide in me," he said awkwardly. "But I think you should know that he sent a radio message yesterday morning."

She turned to look at him, her body tense. "Yes, Simon?" she whispered.

He frowned unhappily, his blue eyes warmly sympathetic. "Oh, damn!" he said desperately. "The message was to Lola Torres. He invited her to join the cruise. He's sending a launch this afternoon to pick her up at Cozumel."

Lola Torres. For a moment Jane couldn't place the name, and then it clicked depressingly. Lola Torres was a very well known personality—though in some circles she was considered more notorious than famous. The gorgeous Spanish-American woman had clawed her way up from the barrios of Los Angeles to become one of the highest-priced call girls in the world, but this hadn't satisfied her. She had wanted to be her own woman, and at twenty-six had written an autobiographical novel entitled, *Kiss and Tell*, wherein she had not only revealed the bedroom secrets of her famous lovers but had had the gall to rate their sexual techniques from one to ten. The book had become a best-seller, and made Lola Torres not only rich but famous. Her warm beauty and razor-sharp wit had made her a favorite on the talk-show circuit.

Jake had definitely brought out the big guns, Jane thought with a pang. He not only intended to show her her own relative unimportance in his life by flaunting another woman before her, but he'd chosen one of the most desirable women in the world to accomplish his aim.

Jane's expression was miserable as she tried to smile at Simon's worried face. "Thank you for telling me, Simon," she said dully. "You're a good friend."

Simon's blue eyes were filled with sympathy as he continued reluctantly, "That's not all, Jane. Captain Benjamin posted a new duty roster last night. You've been replaced as Brockmeyer's helper. Besides acting as Jake Dominic's meal steward, Benjamin has given you duty as Miss Torres's personal maid."

So he not only intended for her to observe his affair with Lola at agonizingly close quarters; he'd placed her quite deliberately in a humiliatingly subservient position to his mistress. He had wanted to hurt her and drive her away, and he'd chosen a method worthy of the Borgias.

She patted Simon's arm comfortingly. "It's all right, Simon." She spoke quietly, with a little ghost of a smile. "Jake's really not being as ruthless as it appears. He probably believes he's being quite benevolent. I'll be fine."

That afternoon as she watched a launch speed across the water toward the *Sea Breeze,* Jane was not quite so confident. At lunch Jake had arrogantly ordered her to be on deck to meet Miss Torres and show her to her cabin. His dark eyes had been alert for any sign of rebellion or distress on her pale heart-shaped face. She would not allow him that victory. She had merely nodded gallantly and carefully assumed a smooth mask to hide the anger and misery this new taunt had caused.

Surprisingly, Kahlid had exhibited a warm sympathy in the brief moment before she had collected the dishes to return to the kitchen. His dark eyes glowing gently, he had leaned closer to whisper in an undertone, "Never mind, *ma petite,* his little flings with the lovely Lola never last more than a week or so. He will soon return to you."

Jane had smiled warmly at the sheik, glad even for this meager comfort. She had murmured a shy farewell in Arabic and quickly left the lounge.

Jake Dominic strolled casually to the rail, his eyes on the approaching launch. He was dressed in close-fitting dark trousers and a gray jacket, a black-and-white ascot knotted around his strong brown throat.

Jake's eyes darted to where Jane waited, her face pale and tense, her body straight and stiff in the steward's uniform. He said in an undertone that only she could hear, "I could order that launch to take you into Cozumel, you know." He continued persuasively. "In two hours you could be on a plane to Miami."

She shook her head silently, her eyes fixed on the launch with strained pain-filled eyes.

There was a flicker of frustration in the dark eyes

as he muttered impatiently under his breath, "Then it's on your head, redhead." His face resumed its usual cynical expression.

Lola Torres was even more ravishing than she was reputed to be, Jane thought wistfully as the launch drew close enough so that she could see the brunette woman standing upright in the boat, her eyes fixed eagerly on Jake Dominic's figure at the rail. Her tall voluptuous body was garbed with understated elegance in black slacks and a white silk blouse that bore the unmistakable cut of a famous French couturier. The long lovely line of her throat was exposed as she tilted her dark silky head back to look at Dominic. Her brilliant smile lit up the olive perfection of her face, and the great dark eyes sparkled eagerly as the launch came alongside.

"Jake, you consummate beast, how dare you summon me like some little harem girl?" she called merrily. "In case you haven't heard, I'm no longer in that business."

Dominic grinned mockingly as he lifted her onto the deck and kissed her lingeringly. "The thought has infinite possibilities, Lola," he said lightly. "You'd make a fantastic harem girl. In six months you'd not only be queen of the seraglio but in all probability you'd be running the country."

Dominic kissed her again on the forehead before turning her around in his arms to face Jane, his hands resting lightly on the woman's waist. "This is Jane Smith, Lola. Knowing what wardrobe you consider minimal, I took the precaution of arranging maid service for you."

There was a look of surprise in Lola Torres's eyes as they met Jane's tormented golden gaze, but her smile was warm. "*Buenas tardes*, Jane. I'm sure that we'll get along very well together."

"Jane will show you to your cabin," Jake went on smoothly as he released her. "I'll see you at dinner, Lola."

Again there was a flicker of puzzlement in Lola's

face, but she nodded agreeably. "As you wish, *querido.*
I am a bit tired."

Jake grinned wickedly, his eyes meeting Jane's
over Lola's satin head. "Be sure you rectify that before you join me for dinner," he said caressingly. "I
want you to be well rested before tonight, Lola."

Jane's eyes blazed with anger at the sheer cruelty
of the taunt, her fists clenching with helpless fury.
She dropped her gaze hurriedly as her eyes met the
shrewd, speculative gaze of the other woman. "If
you'll follow me, Miss Torres, I'll show you to your
cabin." She spoke huskily, trying to blink back the
tears of rage and pain.

"But of course," Lola Torres replied absently, her
eyes still on Jane's unhappy face, and with a final
flashing smile at Jake, she followed Jane's swiftly
moving figure.

The cabin that Lola Torres had been allocated was
only a short distance from Jake's, Jane noticed
morosely. Though smaller than the master cabin, it
was a good size, and the decor was clearly aimed at
pleasing a woman's taste. The thick carpet was a
dusty rose, and the white satin spread on the bed
and the cream velvet Queen Anne occasional chairs
were elegant.

Jane opened the adjoining door to show the older
woman the pretty pink vanity and shower area, before crossing to the porthole and throwing it open to
let in the fresh coolness of the ocean breeze.

"Your luggage will be brought down shortly, Miss
Torres," Jane said with an effort, trying not to look
at the warm beauty whom Jake had so recently held
in his arms. "I'll unpack for you as soon as they
arrive."

"Call me Lola," the other said casually, closing the
door and crossing to the bed to stretch out on the
white satin coverlet. "Sit down and talk to me, Jane."
Her eyes were fixed searchingly on Jane's vulnerable
face. "Now, I want to know what game Jake is playing.
Will you tell me?"

Jane smiled ruefully. Those gorgeous black eyes

evidently concealed a perceptiveness that was positively intimidating. "Jake knows that I love him," she confessed simply, surprising even herself with her frankness. Perhaps it was the gentle warmth that Lola exuded that made her so easy to confide in.

"Yes, he would realize that in short order," Lola said impatiently. "You're fairly transparent." She bit her lip in perplexity. "But Jake usually doesn't find it amusing to be cruel to those who develop an infatuation with him. He merely ignores them. He was really quite vicious to you up on deck."

"He wants to send me back to college," Jane explained quietly. "I don't intend to go."

Lola nodded, comprehension lighting her eyes. "So he sends for me to discourage you," she said wryly. "It's not the greatest compliment I have received."

Jane rushed to reassure her. "It's a very great compliment, Lola." Her tone was earnest. "Who else could show me, just by comparison, how inadequate I am. You're quite a woman."

Lola smiled gently. "You're a generous child, aren't you? I can see why Jake is going to so much trouble over you." Her face was serious as she continued. "He's quite right, you know. He's much too tough and ruthless for a nice infant like you."

Jane shrugged. "Sometimes you can't pick and choose the things that are good for you. Sometimes things just happen." She smiled sadly. "If Jake had to choose anyone to try to discourage me, I'm glad it was you, Lola." She stood up and walked to the door. "I'll go and see what's holding up your luggage."

Jake wouldn't have been pleased at the result of his Machiavellian machinations. Far from being aggravated, Jane's agony and jealousy were inexpressibly soothed by her forced association with Lola Torres. Though both women avoided any further conversation of a personal nature, they got along quite companionably in the hours preceding dinner.

As Jane had expected, this period of tranquillity was to be shattered that evening at dinner. In honor of Lola Torres's arrival, both Jake Dominic and Ahmet Kahlid wore white dinner jackets and a black tie, while the lady herself was lushly alluring, in an orange chiffon gown that clung lovingly to each generous curve.

Brockmeyer had outdone himself to provide an epicurean delight fit for the gods. The table was set with Royal Doulton china and fine white damask linen, and lit by soft, romantic candlelight. These accoutrements formed an ironically civilized background for Jake's ruthless campaign to savage Jane's raw emotions.

He was nothing if not thorough in his tactics, Jane thought almost hysterically at the end of dinner. He was absolutely charming and unfailingly attentive to Lola and coldly impersonal and brisk with her. He spoke only once to Jane during dinner, giving her a curt order to refill Miss Torres's wineglass.

As the meal progressed, Jake's sexual innuendos as he lingeringly caressed the Spanish-American woman became almost too much for Jane to bear. It was with heartfelt relief that she finished serving the after-dinner coffee and prepared to leave the lounge. But it seemed that she wasn't to be allowed even that small mercy.

Jake looked up with the sharp eyes of a hawk as she was walking quietly toward the door. "Wait, Jane," he ordered peremptorily as the trio rose from the table. His eyes were fiercely mocking as he said softly, "I think you had better stay. We may need something."

Jane's golden eyes held the same dumb misery as an animal in pain when she returned his mocking look. She swallowed hard and turned back obediently.

Lola Torres cast a shrewd glance at Jane's shadowed face and then placed a caressing hand on Jake's sleeve. "Send her away, *querido*," she murmured, pouting seductively. "You know I'm not at all fond of sharing the attention of handsome men."

There was a flash of displeasure in Jake's eyes before he smiled down at Lola's entreating face. "She would hardly qualify as competition for you, Lola," he said silkily. "She's only here for your convenience."

Jane flinched as if she had been struck, and she grew even paler. How much more of this could she survive? she wondered desperately.

Unexpectedly, Ahmet Kahlid came to her rescue. "Send the little one away, Jake," he said gallantly, his teeth flashing white in his bearded face. "I wish to wait on this enchanting creature myself. Who knows? By the time the evening is over, she may discover that I'm far more irresistible than you."

Jake frowned and opened his mouth to protest, but Jane had taken advantage of Ahmet's first plea to slip quietly out the door.

She felt passionately grateful to Kahlid for his intervention. She didn't know how she would have been able to tolerate another thirty minutes of Jake Dominic's refined torture. She scurried swiftly away, putting a safe distance between herself and the lounge, almost as though she expected Jake to appear in pursuit.

Like an animal searching for a secluded place to tend its wounds, she hid on a deserted deck, curling up in a deck chair to gaze out at the serenity of the silver-streaked sea. She stayed there for a long time, trying to banish the memory of the evening and to regain the strength of will that Jake had almost destroyed. How was she to last through the days ahead? she wondered despairingly. She would. She must. But, fresh from the agony of Jake's rejection, it seemed a herculean task.

When she had finally composed herself somewhat, she reluctantly left her peaceful haven and made her way to her cabin. She would take a long hot shower and go to bed, she thought resolutely. Perhaps if she tried very determinedly, she would be able to forget the thought of Lola in Jake's bed and find the welcome oblivion of sleep.

Unfortunately, this was not to be the case. After the hot shower she was more wide awake than ever. She changed to her shorty pajamas and flicked off the light. She was about to slip beneath the covers when there was a knock at the door. She frowned in puzzlement and then relaxed. It must be Simon checking to see how she had weathered the evening.

"I'll be right there," she called, and grabbed the matching polka-dot robe. It offered very little protection, as it also came only to her thighs, but at least it covered the transparency of the gown. She turned the light back on and padded barefoot to the door.

It was not Simon. Ahmet Kahlid stood at the door, still dressed in his dazzling white dinner jacket. He held a bottle of champagne in one hand and two champagne glasses in the other. His dark eyes were sparkling brightly, and there was a genial smile on his face.

His gaze roamed frankly and appreciatively over her scantily clad body. "How very alluring you are in that, *ma petite*," he boomed cheerfully. "You look like a young dryad."

She peeked up at him warily. "I was just about to go to bed," she said carefully. "I'm afraid you'll have to excuse me."

He shook his head stubbornly, his smile not losing a bit of its conviviality. "I most certainly will not excuse you," he said breezily. "I couldn't bear to think of you alone and brooding in your cabin. You must have a glass of this most excellent champagne with me so that you will feel happier."

"I appreciate your concern, but I really couldn't—" The rest of her sentence was lost, as Jane was forced to move quickly aside to avoid being trampled by Kahlid when he stepped into the cabin and looked around the room appraisingly.

"How can you breathe in this cabin?" he asked wonderingly. "I can hardly turn around." He put the glasses on the night table and sat down casually on the bed. He patted it invitingly and said softly, "Come and have your champagne, *ma petite*, and soon all your pain will bubble gently away."

Jane closed the door and came forward to sit gingerly on the bed beside him. She didn't want to offend the sheik by refusing the comfort he offered. He had been very sympathetic today, and she was grateful for the help he'd extended tonight in getting her out of the lounge.

"I'll just have one glass, then," she said quietly.

"Good," Kahlid answered approvingly, and he opened the champagne and poured the frothy liquid into the crystal glasses. "You will see that I am right," he continued gently. "It is never good to be alone when one is unhappy."

Jane sipped the champagne slowly, liking the tart taste tingling on the tip of her tongue. Perhaps Kahlid was right at that, she thought. She certainly felt better than she had earlier in the evening. There was something oddly soothing about the big friendly Arab.

"It's very good champagne," she offered, smiling shyly. "But shouldn't you return to Jake and Miss Torres?"

He shook his head ruefully. "I'm very much afraid I was *de trop*. Jake has no desire for a third party when he is with a beautiful woman."

Jane bit her lip and lowered her eyes unhappily.

Kahlid made an impatient gesture. "What a fool I am. Forgive me, little Jane, I did not think." He poured some more champagne into her glass and then set the bottle on the table. "He is an idiot, my friend Jake," he went on gently. "Lola is a very desirable woman, but you have something special, Jane."

Jane stared at him, mesmerized by the intentness in the liquid darkness of Kahlid's eyes. Kahlid, too, was so absorbed that he did not hear the quiet opening of the door.

"Cozy. Very cozy," Jake Dominic said with savage sarcasm. "I must compliment you on your progress, Ahmet, but did you notice that bed is a bit too narrow for a successful seduction?"

Kahlid and Jane both looked up, startled, at Jake standing in the open doorway. He was still dressed in the white dinner jacket, but he had removed the black tie, and his white shirt was left unbuttoned at the throat. His dark hair was slightly rumpled, giving him the look of a rakish pirate. His face, too, had the taut ruthlessness and the blazing fury of a buccaneer about to be deprived of his prize.

Ahmet took one look at that cool deadly anger and instinctively moved away from Jane.

His tone was jovial, but his dark eyes were wary as he said flippantly, "Jake, my friend, you are most unwelcome. I thought I left you very well occupied, and yet here you are interfering with my own pleasure." He shrugged. "I will, however, be magnanimous and offer you a glass of your own champagne before you leave."

Jake Dominic's eyes were molten coals as his gaze took in the two champagne glasses and the half-empty bottle. "You don't usually have to get your women drunk to make them willing, Ahmet."

"She's not drunk," Kahlid said indignantly. "She merely needed soothing after the most unnatural way you savaged the poor *petite* tonight."

Jane shook her head to clear it of both the champagne and the sudden shock of Jake's appearance. "Please, won't you both go away?" she said huskily. "I can't take much more of this."

"You see?" Kahlid charged unhappily. "You have completely spoiled the mood, Jake. Now, go away, and I'll try to repair the damage you have done."

"I'm afraid you'll have to be the one to leave, Ahmet." Jake spoke with deadly softness. "I thought I'd made it clear that Jane was out of bounds."

Kahlid smiled genially. "But that was before you imported the lovely Miss Torres for your pleasure. You made it quite obvious that you were finished with your little servant girl, so why should I not enjoy her?" he asked with utmost reasonableness. "You're not one for a *ménage à trois*, Jake, so don't be like a dog in a manger."

Jake's lips tightened, and his eyes flashed dangerously. "You're wrong, Ahmet, I'm not finished with her. I've barely begun. You'd be wise to leave us before I forget that you're my guest."

Kahlid rose slowly to his feet, his face composed. "As you wish. I have no desire to insult my host by trespassing on what is his." His dark eyes were reproachful. "It was a natural mistake. How was I to know you were so possessive of the girl? You should have made your desires more clear."

"I assure you that from now on my desires will be crystal-clear," Dominic said between his teeth, his furious eyes on Jane's bewildered face and flimsily clad figure. "Now, get the hell out of here before I lose what control I still possess."

Kahlid gave Jane one last regretful glance and moved toward the door. As he passed Jake Dominic's taut, relentless figure, he paused and said calmly, "In order to avoid further confusion, may I ask if Miss Torres is also in the same category?"

Dominic shrugged, his burning eyes fixed on the small red-haired figure on the bed. "Lola may do as she wishes," he said disinterestedly. "Just make damn sure you stay away from Jane!"

The speculation in Ahmet Kahlid's eyes changed to satisfaction. "Well, that is something, at least," he said philosophically. His doleful face was brightening by the second as he went through the open door and closed it gently behind him.

Jane was suddenly conscious of the brevity of her gown and matching robe under the scorching black eyes, which seemed to strip her with insulting thoroughness. She tucked her legs beneath her on the bed and folded her arms around herself with an involuntary shiver as she met Jake's scathing glance across the room.

Then she raised her chin defiantly as the sheer gall of Jake's action came home to her. How dare he come bursting in here, expelling Kahlid without so much as a by your leave, after his own heartless behavior earlier in the evening! It didn't matter that she had been relieved and grateful to him a few minutes ago for ridding her of Kahlid and an extremely touchy situation. For all Jake knew, she may have wanted Ahmet to stay, she thought indignantly. Yet Jake had arrogantly sent him away and now was looking at her with all the possessive fury of a jealous husband. Dog in the manger indeed, she thought grimly.

"If I were you, I'd get that defiant expression off my face pretty damn quick, Jane." His soft voice was menacing. "In case you haven't noticed, I'm a little perturbed with you."

"How very unfortunate for you," Jane said non-chalantly. "There seems to be no pleasing you, Jake." She took a sip of champagne and looked up to meet his gaze with blazing golden eyes. "You may have been able to intimidate Ahmet Kahlid, but you'll find I'm not so easily impressed." She gestured toward the door. "Why don't you go back to the lounge? I'm sure your friend is even now 'poaching' on your preserves."

Dominic's eyes narrowed dangerously. "Champagne courage, Jane?" he asked harshly. "If so, I think you've had enough." He moved across the few feet separating them in a pantherish stride. He took the glass from her hand and set it on the night table.

He looked down at her mutinous face, his eyes glowing with rage. "How did you dare let him come to you?" he said thickly. "I came close to killing the bastard."

Jane caught her breath as a jolt of electricity charged through her at the intensity of his words, his voice. She lowered her eyes and answered eva-sively. "Ahmet was right. How could he know that it mattered to you? Wasn't the whole exercise today designed to get rid of me? What difference does it make if I leave the ship or get involved with some other man? The result would be the same."

He tangled his hand in her hair and jerked her head back so that she was forced to meet the flam-ing possession in his eyes. "Believe me, it makes a difference," he said, his voice tight. "I didn't drive myself crazy trying to keep my hands off you, only to have you drop like a ripe plum into Ahmet's bed."

"You've probably seen to it that it won't be Kahlid,"

she said softly, some perversity tempting her to taunt him. "But what happens after I leave? What's to keep me from jumping into bed with the next likely prospect who crosses my path?" She met his eyes challengingly. "You gave me a taste of the fruit of knowledge. You can't expect me to stop at just a bite."

Dominic's hand tightened; she felt a flicker of fear at the wildness she'd unleashed in the man looking down at her.

"You damn red-haired witch!" he growled thickly, "you'll belong to no one but me!"

His mouth covered hers with the burning brutality of a brand, stamping his possession on the softness of her lips with the explosive passion of a man driven too far. His lips left hers only to press hot, hungry kisses on her throat, cheeks, and lids before returning to her mouth as if starved for the feel of it.

"God knows, I tried to send you away," he said raggedly, between the deliriously sensual kisses that made her feel as if she were slowly melting from the fire they built in her veins.

His arms went around her, lifting and straining her flimsily clad body to his warm hardness, while his lips continued their ruthless pillaging. "I knew damn well that if I kept you around I wouldn't be able to stop myself from having you. Why the hell didn't you leave when you had the chance?"

Her hands slid slowly around his neck, her lips opening and her tongue striving to return the fire he was lighting inside her. He made a sound deep in his throat that was primal in intensity, and she could feel his aroused body tremble against her own.

Suddenly he thrust her away. Jane stared in dazed bewilderment at his flushed face and dark eyes, which were glazed with desire.

"Kiss me, Jake. Please!" she whispered achingly, her body trying to nestle closer to him.

"God! Don't look at me like that or I'll take you right here on this blasted nun's bed." Closing his eyes against the invitation in hers, a great shudder shook his taut body. Suddenly his eyes flew open, and there was purpose in their dark depths.

"Come along!" he ordered curtly, swinging her off the bed and onto her feet. Grasping her by the wrist, he moved across the cabin and opened the door. He strode along the deck and down the stairs, pulling her along behind him.

"Jake, I'm not even dressed!" she cried.

He opened the door of his cabin and ushered her in ahead of him, then shut the door and locked it before turning to flick on the light. Jane gazed at him, her eyes wide, a curiously expectant expression on her heart-shaped face.

His dark eyes shuttered, Jake leaned against the door and regarded her mockingly. "Having second thoughts?" he asked. "It's too late for that, redhead. I'm not going to let you go again."

She felt a wave of shyness wash over her under that mocking gaze. She wished he'd take her in his arms again. She felt no shyness or discomfort when he was making love to her, only the throbbing need and the ecstasy of being close to him.

She lowered her eyes and whispered, "No second thoughts. I want you to make love to me, Jake."

Impulsively he took a step toward her, his hands reaching out to bring her into his arms. He stopped before he touched her, and shook his head ruefully. "Not yet. Once I begin, I'm not going to be able to stop. I don't want your first time to turn you off." His dark eyes gleamed mockingly. "I intend for there to be many more."

He moved away from the door, shrugged off his white jacket, and placed it on a hanger in the closet. He turned back to her, his hands slowly unbuttoning his white shirt while his eyes went over her in frank enjoyment. "Remind me to buy you something more sophisticated in nightwear," he said casually. "That outfit makes me feel like a child molester."

Jane turned away and gingerly sat down on the black-velvet-covered bed, feeling suddenly inadequate. What was she doing here? she wondered desperately.

He was used to the most talented and versatile lovers in the world. Jake Dominic was bound to find her inexperience laughable.

She turned to look at him, her golden eyes troubled. "Jake, what do you want with me?"

He chuckled, his dark eyes dancing, as he pulled his shirt out of his trousers and stripped it off. "Trust a woman to ask a question whose answer is so blatantly self-evident." His expression turned thoughtful. "No, that isn't what you mean, is it?" He stepped out of his shiny black dress shoes. "How long did you think I could say no to you?" he asked quietly. "No one in his right mind would describe me as having a taste for self-sacrifice, and I'm quite obsessed with you. You obviously want to play at being in love with me and to taste what life as Jake Dominic's mistress is like." He smiled cynically. "This will probably be the quickest way of showing you what a mistake you're making." He padded over to where she sat on the bed, and his hand lightly caressed the curve of her cheek. "It will certainly be the most pleasurable way for me."

Her golden eyes clung to his as she rubbed her cheek against his hand like an affectionate kitten. "I do love you," she insisted quietly. She smiled tenderly into the dark intensity of his face. "It's only fair to warn you that you won't get rid of me easily."

For a moment there was an odd vulnerability in the depths of Jake's eyes, before it was replaced by the familiar mockery. "I think I have a fairly accurate idea of what makes you tick, redhead." His voice was tinged with bitterness. "I'll be willing to wager that in a month's time you'll be running for your life."

Jane's eyes met his with such glorious serenity that he caught his breath. "You'll lose," she whispered. "Believe me, you'll lose."

Her small hands reached out to caress the bronze, hair-roughened bareness of his chest. The wiry hair on her sensitive palms generated a deliciously sensual tingle. "You'll have to tell me what to do," she said huskily. "Am I supposed to be getting undressed or something?"

He looked down at her inquiring hands, which were now gently teasing his hard male nipples. "I'd say you're doing pretty well without instructions," he said dryly, his crooked eyebrow arching with humor. "As for the other, I've always had a fondness for opening my own surprise packages."

"I'll turn out the lights," she said with breathless shyness, and made a move to rise.

His hands curved around her shoulders and gently pushed her back on the bed. "No way!" His voice was hoarse. "I want to see every inch of you." He lowered his lips to plant a kiss on the tip of her nose. "One expects such privileges from one's mistress." His hands were gone from her shoulders, and he reached over and snapped on the bedside lamp before moving to the wall switch and turning out the overhead light. He returned to sit beside her on the bed, and with infinitely gentle hands he pulled her carefully into his arms.

He felt so good, so hard, so male, Jane thought as she nestled into his arms like a homing pigeon. Her arms encircled his shoulders to knead and caress the muscles of his back with a sensual pleasure in the feel of their tensile strength.

She became suddenly aware that Jake's body was oddly still and taut as his hands caressed her back slowly and carefully. "Be still a moment, love. I've been wanting this so long that I'm about to explode."

She tried to obey, but he was too close, and she loved him too much. Her eager hands fluttered eagerly over his neck. Her lips brushed teasingly at the hollow of his shoulder before she placed a hundred butterfly kisses on the warm hard flesh of his chest and shoulders.

"You little devil." He chuckled raggedly, his heart beating like a triphammer beneath her mouth. He lifted her quickly to cradle her on his knees. "So much for exercising restraint with my little virgin," he said thickly. "Oh, well, there's always the second time."

His lips once more covered hers, and all thought of restraint was a thing of the past. She felt that the hot obsessive pressure of his mouth was absorbing her into his every muscle and bone by the simple process of melting her own body with a flaming need for him. His tongue licked teasingly at her lips before entering to explore her inner sweetness, his hands curving around her to cup her breasts in his hands through the thin material of her gown. She trembled at the heat from his hands, which weighed and toyed erotically with her breasts while his tongue ruthlessly plundered her mouth.

Then, with his mouth still probing hers, his hands were working at her robe, slipping her arms out of the sleeves and letting it fall discarded across his knees. His hands moved under the top to caress the sensitive line of her satiny back with feverish hunger. His lips left hers to bury themselves in her throat, while his hands slid around to play with the naked bounty of her small pert breasts, his thumbs flicking the nipples till they were hard with arousal. "I've got to see you, sweetheart," he groaned, and with one swift movement he pulled the baby-doll top over her head and threw it carelessly on the floor. She was wearing only the bikini bottom as he swept her over to lie in the center of the ebony velvet counterpane.

He lay above her, his weight resting on one elbow while he stared raptly at the lovely silken flesh bared to his gaze. Bending to take one rosy nipple in his mouth, he teased it with maddening skill until her breath was coming in little pants, as though she had been running. Her hands went around his neck to bury themselves in his hair and bring him closer, but he pulled away.

His hands cupped her breasts, his eyes clouded with desire. "Your breasts were designed to fit into my hands," he said hoarsely. "After the night you spent in my cabin, I'd lie awake and think of you lying like this under me, your breasts warm and rosy from my kisses. It nearly drove me crazy." His heart was beating wildly as he bent and rubbed his chest sensually against her bare breasts. She shuddered beneath him, and her arms tightened convulsively around him.

Then he was gone for a minute while he stripped off the remainder of his clothes. When he returned, the warmth of his naked flesh was dizzily exciting against her own.

What followed was a breathtaking spiral of sensation that she embraced with incredulous joy. Jake brought her from peak to peak with touch and tongue and with wild words that were an aphrodisiac in themselves.

She followed blindly, while he moved her, aroused her, built in her a frantic need that she was sure could not be satisfied. Then he set about proving her wonderfully and ecstatically wrong. If there was pain, she was not aware of it, so involved was she in reaching that summit that beckoned like a pot of gold at the end of the rainbow's spectrum of sensual sensation. When she did reach it, she discovered, after the first explosion of wonder and delight, that it was not a glittering treasure after all, but the deeper, primitive satisfaction of coming home.

She wriggled contentedly in Jake's arms, her heartbeat steadying as she felt a delicious languor attack her limbs. Jake's arms tightened automatically around her, his breathing still coming in short gasps, his heartbeat thudding beneath her ear with the delicious proof of his own excitement at their union.

She kissed the smooth muscled shoulder lovingly. Then she raised herself on one elbow to look down at him with frank enjoyment. He was so beautiful, she thought with a new pride of possession. The magnificent bone structure that was the basis of his good looks was generally overlooked, so exciting were the mobility and expressiveness of his face. Now, with his eyes closed and his face relaxed, Jane could see the beauty of line and contour that would make him devastatingly handsome even in old age.

His eyes flicked open and lit with mocking amusement as they met the serious expression in Jane's eyes. "What are you thinking, redhead?" he asked curiously as his hand reached up lazily to trace the line of her shoulder.

"I was thinking what a distinguished old man you'll make," she said dreamily.

He pulled her down to kiss her lingeringly. "I'd rather you concentrate on my present attractions and talents," he said, grinning wickedly. He settled her head back in the hollow of his shoulder, his hand stroking her red curls gently.

"Would you like for me to get you a cigarette?" she asked suddenly.

"A cigarette?" Jake asked blankly.

"I thought all men wanted a cigarette after . . ." She paused delicately.

"It's optional," he assured her solemnly.

She accepted that, and after another blissfully lazy moment, another thought occurred to her. "You said you only smoke in stressful situations," she said curiously. "You don't consider this a stressful situation?"

His lips brushed the top of her head tenderly before lifting her chin to meet his eyes with surprising seriousness. "I consider this situation a delight!" He kissed the tip of her nose. "I consider it sheer enchantment!" He kissed her forehead. "I consider it a miracle!" His lips tasted hers with a blinding sweetness.

"Oh, so do I," Jane said enthusiastically, when their lips finally parted. She impulsively pressed her lips to his once more, eager to experience once again that melting tenderness.

Jake's eyes were dancing with amusement when their lips parted for the second time. "I'm glad that your first experience met with your approval," he said, his lips twitching. "I gather you have no regrets about your fall from grace?"

She shook her head tranquilly, her eyes shining with tenderness. "I regard it as falling into grace. Love in itself must be the ultimate in grace." She kissed him gently. "I could never regret loving you, Jake Dominic."

His face was unreadable as he stared into her glowing, eager face. "No tears, no demands, no guilt trips," he said slowly. "You make it ridiculously easy to take advantage of you, redhead."

She giggled happily and put her head back into the spot in the hollow of his shoulder that was becoming endearingly familiar. "It is I who am taking advantage of you," she said teasingly. "You're the one with all the experience. I'm just a humble novice. It's only sensible to keep you sweet, so that you're inclined to continue the lessons."

"You'll have no problem on that score," he said dryly. "I'm having to remind myself right now that you're new at this game and mustn't be overworked."

She lifted her head to stare into his face. "Already?" she asked, startled.

"Already," he affirmed, his dark eyes twinkling mischievously. "I have an idea that you're a born voluptuary, Jane. I'm eager to test the theory."

Suddenly his eyes lost their mockery and began to burn with a flame that she had already known once tonight. The world seemed to narrow into dark velvet intimacy, and she felt her own heartbeat accelerate in response to that evocative memory.

"I'm not that sore," she whispered breathlessly.

It was all he needed to hear. He rolled her over on her back, his warm, virile body a powerful shadow above her. "I'm afraid the results would be the same even if you were," he muttered thickly. "I'll try to be gentle, sweetheart."

"It doesn't matter," she said softly, her hands moving yearningly over his shoulders.

"Yes, it does," he denied huskily as his lips hovered lingeringly over hers. "The first time was for me, redhead. This one is for you."

Nine

She was lying in a field of flowers, the sun caressing her cheeks with its golden warmth. A gentle breeze blew the silken petals of the wild flowers in an occasional drifting kiss across her face. She smiled in childlike pleasure at the lovely sensual sensation and arched her throat to expose more of her flesh to that delicious touch.

"Open your eyes, redhead," Jake said softly. "I want to make damn sure that smile is for me."

Jane opened drowsy eyes to see Jake leaning over her, his dark eyes narrowed in amusement and, incredibly, a touch of jealousy. The early-morning sunlight streamed into the cabin, revealing the sharp lines of cynicism and weariness around his mouth.

Her hands reached up dreamily to trace the grooves with gentle fingers. "It's for you," she said simply. "Everything is for you."

"It had better be," Jake growled as he nuzzled at the hollow of her throat. "I'd best warn you that I'm feeling surprisingly possessive of you, woman. I doubt if I'd tolerate your straying while you belong to me."

He didn't see the sudden flicker of pain in her eyes at that last remark. She had forgotten, in the breathless pleasure of belonging to Jake, the transient nature of their relationship. It was obvious from his casual statement that he had not been so blinded. Well, what had she expected? she asked herself impatiently. Jake was not about to display the same love-struck idiocy as she. She must learn to accept what Jake had to offer and be satisfied, expecting no more.

He had raised his head at the involuntary stiffening of her body, and his eyes took on a ruthless hardness. "I'm sorry if you don't approve of the terms," he said coolly. "You'll just have to submit to them if you intend to remain my mistress."

She half closed her eyes to mask the misery they revealed. "You don't have a reputation for demanding such fidelity," she commented lightly.

He shrugged and rolled away from her. He rested on one elbow, his hand playing idly with her curls. "Perhaps it's because I was the first," he suggested mockingly. "I feel quite primitive at the thought of anyone else having you."

"And will you give me the same fidelity?" she asked clearly.

"For the present," he said lazily. "I imagine I'll find you more than satisfying for some time to come."

"And Lola Torres?" she asked quietly.

"I owe Lola nothing," he said with casual callousness. "She understood why she was here. She'll understand why she's no longer needed. I'll send her away today."

Jane sat upright in bed, her eyes blazing indignantly. "You can't do that," she protested. "How would she feel? You can't just snap your fingers one day and have her fly thousands of miles to join you and then just say you've changed your mind. She'd be terribly hurt."

Dominic's lips quirked with humor. "What do you suggest I do? I doubt if I'd have the stamina to satisfy another woman after you," he said mischievously. "My new mistress seems to require all my energy." He reached out to cup one enticing breast, which had been bared by her abrupt movement.

Jane brushed his hand away impatiently and pulled the covers up around her, tucking the material under her armpits to hold it in place. "Don't be ridiculous. I'd probably claw her eyes out if you so much as looked at her. I just think that you should let her make the move to go. It will let her keep her dignity."

Jake grinned, his eyes mocking. "You're very solicitous of Lola's feelings. She's tougher than you could ever be, my little crusader. It goes with the territory."

"I'm sure she was forced by circumstances into that kind of life," Jane replied in defense, her face flushing with the force of her conviction. "And whatever she did, I'm sure it was with dignity. She's more courtesan than call girl."

"A delicate distinction, I agree," he said solemnly, his dark eyes twinkling. "All right, redhead, I'll let Lola make the decision to leave." He chuckled, shaking his head ruefully. "And to think that I was trying to protect your feelings by ridding myself of a former mistress." He touched the tip of her nose with one finger. "Do me one favor. Don't try to mother Lola. She would find it most uncomfortable."

Jane gave him an indignant glance. Why did he insist on believing that she was some sort of Joan of Arc just because she displayed concern for someone's feelings? She hadn't really been in trouble since the incident at the cockfight. Well, there had been the shark, but even he couldn't blame her for that.

Pulling the cover around her, she began to scoot to the edge of the bed.

"Where do you think you're going, sweetheart?" Jake asked, watching her try to hold the sheet under her arm and still wrap the rest of it around her slight body.

"I've got to report to work."

Jake suddenly reached over and hauled her protesting body back to the center of the bed. "My dear idiot Jane, you have no work to go to. Didn't it occur to you that it would be a trifle awkward to be both my mistress and my steward?"

"I don't see why," Jane said, pouting mutinously.

"Kahlid and the crew already have accepted the situation!"

"I don't give a damn about Kahlid or the crew," he said deliberately, annoyance flickering in his face. "I don't want to have to come looking for you every time I want you. It seems you need instructions in the nuances of being a mistress. Perhaps you should have a talk with Lola."

She flushed at the cruelty of the jibe but persisted nevertheless. "Perhaps we could arrange a schedule," she suggested seriously.

Dominic gave a derisive laugh. "No way!" he said emphatically. "Jane, I'll give you any damn thing you want. All I ask is that you make yourself available when I want to be with you. Is that too much to ask?"

Jane could see his viewpoint. In his eyes her reluctance to comply with his request must seem completely unreasonable. She wondered if he'd ever known a woman who preferred menial work to the sybaritic and sensual pleasures he offered.

Her golden eyes were troubled, as she pleaded hesitantly, "Couldn't we go on just as we have been?" Then, as he looked at her blankly, she blushed and rushed on hurriedly. "Except for this, of course." She made a vague gesture indicating themselves and the bed. "I don't really think I'd be happy without some work to do. I'm used to being independent."

For a moment she thought she could read understanding and sympathy in Jake's eyes before he glanced away. "I'm afraid I couldn't allow that," he said, his voice hard. "You should have realized there would be aspects of our relationship that you'd find distasteful before you committed yourself." His smile was bitter. "It's well known that I'm a selfish bastard."

"But won't you . . ." Jane was suddenly silenced by Jake's lips on hers.

"God save me from an argumentative woman," Jake said thickly. "The only sounds I want to hear from you in the next hour are the delicious little moans you made last night." His hands deliberately pulled the sheet down to her waist and began their magical play on her body. "You also may say 'yes, Jake,' he decreed with a chuckle.

Jane's breath caught in her throat, and she felt the familiar melting in her loins. Her arms slid lovingly around his neck.

"Yes, Jake," she whispered.

It was almost two hours later when Jake phoned and ordered breakfast. At the same time he gave instructions that Jane's belongings be packed and brought to his cabin. Jane did not comment on this embarrassing and arbitrary ordering of her life. However, she disappeared discreetly into the shower shortly before the steward was due to put in his appearance. When she returned to the bedroom draped inelegantly in Jake's wine velour robe, her clothes had been delivered and a portable table had been wheeled in with breakfast.

Jake was seated at the table as she walked into the room. He looked up, his dark eyes knowing. "You can't run away from it indefinitely, you know."

Jane did not pretend to misunderstand him. "I know," she replied, not looking at him as she seated herself opposite him at the table. "I just thought it would be easier to face after the first novelty had worn off. The fact that I've officially moved in with you will be old news by tomorrow."

His lips thinned with anger. "I won't have you made uncomfortable. I'll fire the first man who raises so much as an eyebrow."

Jane smiled wryly as she lifted the silver covers off the various dishes and helped herself to eggs, sausage, and toast. She was surprised that Jake didn't realize that speculation and rumors couldn't be stopped by merely ordering them to. Even though no overt mention or acknowledgment would be made of her new position, she would still be conscious that every man on the *Sea Breeze* knew that she was now Jake Dominic's latest toy. She could not deny even to herself that the thought chafed unbearably at her pride.

When they joined Kahlid and Lola for lunch in the lounge, it was even more awkward for her. Both Kahlid and Lola accepted her presence as a guest instead of an employee with casual aplomb. Jane wished she could rival their composure instead of feeling this agony of shyness and discomfort. She was almost silent through the long lunch, though some of her nervousness was abated by the fact that the attending steward was almost a stranger. She had been worried that Simon would be chosen as her replacement, and she didn't feel she could quite cope with that at the moment.

Jake seemed to feel no awkwardness, and he treated her with a curious blend of mocking indulgence and possessiveness. He ignored her shyness and saw to it that she was included in the conversation by simply changing the subject immediately whenever Lola or Kahlid made reference to something outside her experience.

Jane was touched by the arrogant protectiveness of his attitude, but it only added to her embarassment when she met Lola's amused eyes across the table. The older woman said nothing until Jake and Ahmet Kahlid excused themselves to wander over to the bar. Lola then quietly invited Jane to go for a walk on deck with her.

They were no sooner beyond the door than Lola started to chuckle. "I haven't enjoyed anything so much in years," she drawled, her dark eyes dancing. "The sight of Jake Dominic in the role of shepherd to his lamb was absolutely priceless. That alone was worth the trip from Los Angeles."

Jane gave her a sheepish grin and said wryly, "He did rather overdo it, didn't he? He wasn't exactly tactful to you and Kahlid in his support of me."

"Jake can be the soul of diplomacy if it's called for," Lola said shrewdly. "In this case it wasn't necessary. He knew that Ahmet and I would get the picture."

"Lola, you've been very kind to me," Jane said hesitantly. "I just wanted—"

Lola waved her imperiously to silence. "For God's sake, don't apologize," she said cheerfully. "I would have had to be blind not to realize there was something in the air last night at dinner. Jake has never been known for his kindness to women, but he was completely unreasonable with you. Then, when he discovered Ahmet had gone to your cabin, he was like a madman."

"How did he know that?" Jane asked curiously. It had not occurred to her to question Jake's sudden appearance in her cabin in the tumultuous events that had followed.

"I imagine he'd given orders that he be told if Ahmet was seen going anywhere near your cabin," Lola replied with a shrug. "A steward came with a message for Jake shortly after Ahmet left the lounge. The ungrateful wretch didn't so much as say good night to me before he was off to the rescue."

"I'm sure he didn't *mean* to be rude, Lola."

Lola's lips twisted. "He didn't give a damn what I felt, my dear innocent. The only thing he could think about was you." Her eyes were thoughtful as she studied Jane objectively. "I believe that's all he's been able to think of for quite some time, from his reaction last night. I've never seen Jake with his emotions as well as his hormones involved. Perhaps I should be warning *him* about getting involved, and not you."

Jane knew a surge of hope that lightened the burden of anxiety and doubt she'd been feeling this morning. Was it possible that Jake was beginning to feel something for her besides desire and the urge for possession?

"Is that what you're doing? Warning me? If so, I'm afraid that you're a little late."

"I rather suspected I might be, but I thought I'd give it a try," Lola said, smiling gently. "Now we'd better return you to your lord and master before he comes looking for you."

They turned and retraced their steps to the lounge.

The rest of the day was spent in swimming, lounging, and desultory conversation. Jane found herself restless and dissatisfied despite the happiness she felt in Jake's presence. She was too used to hard work and constant activity to embrace the leisurely life with any degree of contentment. She was conscious of Jake's watchful eyes on her throughout the afternoon though he engaged her in only casual conversation in the presence of the others.

Thus she was only mildly surprised when he strolled casually over to the deck chair where she was lying watching the scarlet-and-pink glory of a sunset at sea. Kahlid and Lola had gone into the water for a last dip before going to their cabins to change for dinner, and she and Jake were alone for the first time since they had left their cabin that morning.

"Poor Saturday's child," Jake said mockingly as he dropped into the chair next to her. "Are you finding it hard to adjust to the lazy life?"

Jane was startled by his perceptiveness. Had her restlessness been so obvious? "I suppose I'll get used to it," Jane said doubtfully. She looked at him, noting the vibrant energy and impatience that seemed to charge his body even in repose. "How do you tolerate it?" she asked ruefully. "I would think the inactivity would drive you crazy."

"I admit that my boredom threshold is very low these days," Jake said. "I probably would have scrapped the cruise after two weeks if I hadn't had a certain troublesome redhead to divert me." He took her hand from the arm of the lounge and, bringing it to his lips, kissed the palm lingeringly.

Jane shivered as his tongue mischievously stroked the sensitive hollow, and he looked up swiftly in concern. He reached over her head to the white beach coat draped on the back of her chair and tossed it on her lap. "Put it on. It's starting to cool."

"That isn't my problem," Jane said demurely, her golden eyes dancing. "I'm beginning to feel definitely hot."

Dominic's dark eyes were amused. "Have you no inhibitions, woman?"

She shook her head. "Where you're concerned, they seem to have been left out of my makeup," she admitted serenely.

"Thank God," Jake said emphatically. His hand held hers tightly as his eyes slowly kindled with desire. "Damn it, why did I let you talk me into letting Lola stay? If she was gone, I could persuade Ahmet that he'd be better off roaming in greener pastures." His thumb sensually rubbed the pulse point at her wrist. "I warn you, redhead, you'd better enjoy the fresh air now," he said thickly. "Once I find a way of getting ridding of them, you may not get out of that cabin for a week."

Jane wondered if he could feel her pulse wildly accelerate beneath his thumb at these words. She rather imagined he could, by the teasing gleam of triumph that glittered in his eyes before she looked away.

"I think I'll go down to the cabin and change now," she said quickly, a flush turning her cheeks carnation pink. She stood up hurriedly and slipped on her beach coat.

Jake arched an eyebrow mockingly at her embarrassed flight. "Inhibitions, no. Shyness, definitely yes." He also got to his feet. "I think I'll join you. I feel the sudden urge for a long nap," he said, his lips twitching. "Do you suppose our guests would understand if we were a little late for dinner?"

"Jake!" she exclaimed, shocked, her eyes widening. He broke into irrepressible laughter, his face suddenly as young and mischievous as a boy's.

Jane was about to take him to task when she suddenly became aware of the jerky throb of a distant engine. She forgot what she was about to say when she saw a gold and white helicopter approaching from the east and progressing unmistakably in their direction.

Jake's laughing eyes followed her startled gaze, and he muttered an impatient imprecation as he caught sight of the helicopter. "What abominably bad timing," he said grimly. The deck was suddenly filled with scurrying, bustling seamen.

"What is happening?" Jane asked blankly, as the helicopter hovered directly overhead, the rotors causing a small tornado of wind and noise.

"A little gift for you," he replied casually. The side doors of the helicopter slid open, and Jane caught a brief glimpse of an olive-uniformed Mexican and then an enormous box and several smaller ones were lowered by net to the surface of the deck below.

"What on earth is it, a refrigerator?" she asked faintly, while the seaman briskly closed in on the net to remove the packages.

Lola Torres joined them, towel-drying her sleek wet head, before slipping on her scarlet beach coat. Jane had been vaguely aware of Lola's return to the deck at the approach of the helicopter. The other woman's face was frankly curious as she eyed the bundles that had now been freed from the net.

In answer to Lola's inquiring look, Jane said with a grin. "Jake's bought me a present. I haven't yet decided whether it's a refrigerator or a washing machine."

Lola examined one of the smaller packages lying on the deck. "I imagine Dior would be most outraged by your flippancy," she said dryly. She picked up another box. "Ditto Balenciaga."

"Jane's luggage was unfortunately left ashore in Miami," Jake put in smoothly "I took the liberty of ordering a replacement wardrobe for her."

Lola gave a little gurgle of laughter. "How simply divine!" Turning to Jane, she said gaily, "A 'present' like this deserves a party. We'll have to arrange something really splendid to celebrate, and I know just the nightclub in Cozumel to do it in!" She turned to Jake and ordered imperiously, "Tell them to hold dinner at least an hour. Jane will need that long just to open the packages."

An hour later, Jane sat dazed on the edge of the bed, staring in amazement at the boxes surrounding her. When she'd opened the huge crate, she had found that it contained two enormous steamer trunks filled with designer clothes of every description along with a shoe wardrobe to match every outfit. The loose packages were principally accessories and lingerie, with the exception of two of the larger boxes. One of these contained a full-length sable coat, and the other an ermine wrap. It was impossible not to be a trifle overwhelmed by the extravagance of Jake's gift. It was every woman's dream to receive a wardrobe of such classic elegance.

Yet how could she accept it and still maintain her self-respect and independence while living with Jake?

"Well, redhead, have you discovered anything that I've missed?" Jake Dominic stood in the open doorway, dressed for dinner in a white tropical jacket and black tie.

Jane didn't answer, and Jake sauntered forward. "You'll notice that I omitted any little baubles from Tiffany's. I prefer Van Cleef and Arpels," he said lazily. "I'll let you choose your own jewelry on our first trip over."

"I won't accept any jewelry, Jake," Jane said slowly, her cheeks pale. "I'll take the clothes because I realize that it might cause you some embarrassment if I didn't maintain a certain appearance, but I won't accept anything else from you."

"I suppose I should have expected something like this from you," Jake answered, his expression darkening ominously. "For your information, I didn't arrange for this wardrobe because I was ashamed of you. I did it because I want to give you a present, and women generally like this sort of thing." His voice was hard: "If you don't want them, throw them into the sea! Throw everything you own into the sea, I prefer you without a stitch anyway!"

Jane stared into his hard, ruthless face and saw something in the dark flickering eyes that she'd never seen before. Why, she had hurt him! She had grown used to thinking of Jake as the hard, cynical sophisticate, but now he had the defiant air of a young boy who had surrendered a treasure to a comrade only to have it scorned. Suddenly she wanted to take him in her arms and soothe away all of the hurts he had ever known. Because she knew that she must never show that she had seen that vulnerability, she dropped her eyes to the amber scarf in her lap.

When she raised them a moment later, her golden eyes were dancing with fun. "I like you better without a stitch, too," she told him, grinning. "I love the clothes, Jake. I'll be very happy to accept them." What was a little pride when it was balanced against the hurt she'd inflicted on the man she loved?

Dominic relaxed, his face regaining its cool insouciance. "Brat," he drawled. "You can't even accept a present without causing a ballyhoo." He strolled over to where she was sitting on the bed and dropped a light kiss on her forehead. "And the jewels?" he probed.

She wasn't willing to give him total victory. "We'll see," she replied evasively. Then looking up quickly, her eyes troubled, she said, "There's one thing that I can't accept, Jake." His face darkened swiftly, and she went on hurriedly, "It's the furs. I could never wear the skin of an animal that had been killed so that I could flaunt its beauty as some kind of status symbol. I just couldn't do it."

Jake's frown faded slowly, to be replaced by resignation. "No, I suppose you couldn't," he said wryly. "Knowing you, I should have realized that would be one of your *bête noires.*"

Her face was serious. "I helped circulate a petition last year to try to get legislation passed against the killing of baby seals. Do you know how they kill baby seals?"

Jake placed a hand over her mouth. "No," he said firmly, "and I don't want to know. At least not before dinner." He removed his hand and tilted her head up to place a swift kiss on her mutinous mouth. "Suppose we send the furs back and use the money as a contribution to your seal fund."

Jane's face lit up with the power of a solar explosion. "Oh, Jake, could we?" she breathed excitedly. "They do need the money so desperately."

"If you promise to send the check in your name and not mine," Jake said, making a face. "I have no desire to be put on the hit list of every wildlife-preservation society in the country."

Jane jumped up and hugged him impulsively. "Jake, you're super. Absolutely super," she bubbled.

Jake flinched, but his arms went around her with swift possessiveness. "Please. Not that word. You make me feel like a rock star." His hands were moving in lazy circles on her lower back and buttocks beneath the beach coat, and Jane felt her knees turn to butter. She pressed closer to him and felt the swift exciting hardening of him against her. He drew a deep ragged breath and pushed her reluctantly away. "Damn Lola and her party," he said thickly. "I'd like nothing better than to tell the whole world to go to hell and spend the evening in bed." He turned away. "Get dressed, redhead. I'll see you in the lounge."

A short time later Jane gazed with breathless delight in the mirror. Why, she looked pretty. The chocolate chiffon cocktail-length gown was a masterpiece of artistic drapery that left one golden shoulder bare, hugging her high firm breasts and tiny waist lovingly before flaring to an extravagant fullness at the scalloped hem. The matching satin high-heeled sandals made her legs look deliciously alluring. Her hair curled in shimmering flames about her face in dramatic contrast to the rich darkness of her gown. Her topaz eyes and the tender pink of her mouth exerted a sensual witchery that Jane had never realized she possessed. The swift kindling in Jake's eyes as she walked into the lounge was as exhilarating and heady as champagne. She barely noticed Kahlid's flattering and verbose compliments as she basked in that ebony glow.

When Jake swung Jane down into the launch, she was surprised to see Marcus Benjamin and Simon Dominic at the wheel in the front of the boat. Impulsively Jane made a sudden movement toward them, and Jake gripped her arm swiftly.

"Over here, darling," he said caressingly, and shepherded her to a seat near the rear of the boat. He settled her so gallantly, so solicitously, that he might just as well have stamped her with a brand of ownership. She could feel her face burn in the darkness as Jake slipped a casual arm about her waist.

Jane had an idea that Jake's actions were as deliberate and primitive as those of a jungle cat staking out its boundaries. Her move toward Simon had been only an innocent impulse, principally aimed at reassuring herself that she still had Simon's respect and friendship despite her position in his cousin's life. Jake had seized on the excuse to establish his public claim with no regard to the embarrassment such an action would bring her. She couldn't help but feel a burning resentment at the inconsiderateness of his action. "I didn't know that Simon and Captain Benjamin were going with us," she said tightly.

"Lola insisted," Jake answered curtly. "She's never happier than when she's surrounded by men—a common feminine characteristic I've noticed."

Jane maintained a cool silence during the forty-minute ride to the pier at Cozumel. Her own reserve went unremarked in the wake of Lola's vivacious gaiety and Kahlid's equally good spirits. Jake seemed maddeningly undisturbed by Jane's disapproval and displayed a lazy good humor that was a barbed irritant to her rapidly deteriorating mood. Her gaze went frequently to the front of the launch, where Captain Benjamin and Simon conversed casually in low voices. Both men wore sparkling white uniforms that compared very favorably with Jake's and Kahlid's white tropical dinner jackets and dark pants, Jane thought idly.

Suddenly Jake's grasp around her waist tightened sharply, and his voice in her ear was a silken murmur. "I've always heard that women were fond of men in uniform," he said caustically. "Don't you think you're being a little obvious in your admiration?"

Jane raised her chin defiantly. "Perhaps I feel an affinity with them," she said with sweet sarcasm. "If you remember, I was wearing a uniform myself until today. There's a certain kindred spirit among us menials, you know."

Dominic's rapier glance was as black as his muttered imprecation, and he was grimly silent for the rest of the trip.

El Invernardero was a thoroughly enchanting nightclub located in the heart of Cozumel. It was a converted greenhouse constructed entirely of paneled glass, and a multitude of exotic plants and flowers bordered the interior walls in colorful profusion. The highly polished dance floor was encircled by the usual damask-covered tables, but on each was a charmingly arranged bouquet of fresh flowers.

Their party was shown to a large ringside table by an obsequious waiter. Jake pulled out a chair beside his own for Jane, but Lola had other ideas.

"Don't be selfish, Jake," she said, her dark eyes sparkling with mischief. "You can have Jane to yourself anytime." She gave Jane an imperious nudge that placed her across the table, between Kahlid and Simon. She herself slid into the seat next to Jake and smiled dazzlingly into his frowning face. "Now, isn't this delightful?"

"Delightful," Jake echoed grimly, his watchful gaze fixed on Kahlid as the sheik helped Jane solicitously with her chiffon wrap.

For Jane, as the evening wore on, what had promised to be an exciting and romantic evening with the man she loved rapidly deteriorated into a miserable debacle. Jake's mood progressed from testy to utterly foul. Separated by the width of the table, Jane was still conscious of the black looks she was receiving as she quietly spoke to Kahlid or Simon. What had she done now to deserve his lordship's displeasure? she wondered defiantly. She turned to Kahlid with a sigh of relief. Ahmet's attitude was beautifully uncomplicated. He cared not a whit for morals, blame, and responsibility as long as he was in the presence of an attractive woman and champagne was flowing. He saw to it that champagne continued to flow throughout the evening, and that Jane's glass was constantly filled to the brim.

As Jane's unhappiness grew, she was grateful for Kahlid's attention. Jake had not asked her to dance once in the hours they had been at the nightclub, though he'd danced frequently with Lola. To add to her misery, a depressingly gorgeous blonde with a face that had graced hundreds of magazine covers and wearing a gown with a neckline even more decolleté than Lola's had suddenly appeared at Jake's elbow. She'd been introduced to everyone at the table. Cindy Lockwood, a model from New York, had attached herself to Jake like a seductive limpet. He had danced with the model even more than he had with Lola, Jane noticed unhappily.

The explosive combination of Cindy Lockwood, her own unhappiness and resentment, and Kahlid's champage sparked a wildness in Jane. She proceeded to ignore Jake entirely, dividing her attention between Kahlid and Simon with feverish gaiety. She didn't know how many times she changed partners in the next two hours as she whirled from Simon's arms to Kahlid's and back.

At one point she found herself dancing with a handsome Latin who held her much too close and murmured romantic Spanish nothings in her ear. She vaguely remembered gaily accepting his invitation to dance when the young man presented himself at their table. His name was Ramon de . . . something or other, and she found that his arms were just as comforting as Kahlid's or Simon's if she couldn't be with Jake.

Then an authorative hand tapped the man on the shoulder, and she looked up to see a grim-faced

Jake beside them. "My dance, I believe," he said crisply, placing his hand at Jane's waist and whisking her firmly into his own embrace.

Ramon frowned crossly, but after a glance at Jake's face, he turned sulkily away.

"Your Latin lover gives up easily," Jake said with a savage grin. "I'm disappointed. I was looking forward to rearranging those classic features."

Jane only half heard him as she nestled closer into his arms, everything forgotten but the blissful fact that she was in Jake's embrace.

"This is the first time we've danced together," she said dreamily as her arms slipped around his neck. "I did so want to dance with you, Jake." Her face clouded. "Then somehow everything was spoiled." She shook her head bewilderedly. It was all too complicated to think about now.

"You seemed to keep yourself well occupied," he said harshly as they moved languidly around the floor. "It was quite fascinating watching you try out your wiles on every man in the room. Did you enjoy yourself, Delilah?"

"No," she said simply, her cheek rubbing gently back and forth on his white linen shoulder. "I only wanted you." She looked up into his face with pleading eyes. "Take me home, Jake."

He looked down at her, his face expressionless except for the flickering flame in his dark eyes. "Champagne appears to make you quite amorous, my little sex kitten. By all means, let's go back to the yacht. After all, it's my privilege to end the evening with you, regardless of how many men you require to keep you contented." He stopped dancing in the middle of the room and turned away abruptly. Grasping her by the wrist, he strode through the dancers toward the front door of the nightclub.

"Where are we going?" Jane gasped, trying to keep pace with his long-legged stride.

"We're going back to the yacht, where else?" he replied mockingly. "You want to be alone with me, remember?"

A nagging uneasiness pierced the golden haze induced by the champagne, like the first rays of sunlight through the morning fog. "But we can't just run off and leave the others without saying a word."

They had reached the street now, and at Jake's imperious motion, the red-liveried doorman summoned a taxi with his piercing silver whistle.

"I don't see why not," Jake said coolly. "We'll send the launch back for them."

He bundled her into the taxi and climbed in after her with a curt order in Spanish to the cab driver.

Jane shivered as her bare shoulder touched the cold vinyl of the upholstery. "My wrap," she said vaguely, "I left my wrap at the table."

"Someone will bring it," Jake said indifferently. His arm slid around her, and he pulled her closer to the heat of his own vibrant body.

Jane rested her head in the curve of his shoulder. She was conscious even in the intimacy of the embrace that his hold was strangely impersonal, and the knowledge would have troubled her if she hadn't suddenly been overcome with drowsiness.

Her next recollection was of being lifted into the launch and wrapped in Jake's white dinner jacket, which smelled deliciously of starch and shaving lotion. Then, after another brief period of sleep, she was aware of being carried in Jake's arms and placed on the unmistakable softness of a bed.

Jane opened her eyes drowsily to see Jake straightening slowly, his dark face shuttered. She looked around the master cabin of the *Sea Breeze* with a sigh of contentment. How strange that this luxurious suite had so quickly become home to her, she thought dreamily. Even the grotesque graffiti on the wall opposite the bed brought forth only an affectionate smile.

"I'm glad you're back with me, sleeping beauty," Jake said teasingly, "and in such a good mood, too."

She turned and smiled happily at him, admiring the tough masculine grace of the rippling muscles in his chest and shoulders as he stripped off the white dress shirt and threw it carelessly on the gray velvet chair across the room.

She came into his arms like a nail to a magnet when he sat down beside her on the bed. Her lips brushed his throat in a multitude of soft, yearning kisses.

His arms held her quietly. "Such a loving, passionate nature," he said coolly, pushing her away to look down at her with narrowed eyes. "I wonder how much of it is for me alone." His forefinger idly traced the full curve of her lower lip. "Would you fly just as eagerly into young Simon's arms, now that I've shown you the way?"

She looked up at him, her golden eyes clouded with bewilderment. "I don't understand."

"That was more than obvious tonight," he said softly as his hands left her shoulders and moved down her back to deftly unzip the chiffon gown. "But I have every intention of making sure that everything is quite clear to you by morning."

He unfastened the strapless bra and pushed it, with her dress, to her waist. His dark head bent slowly, and his lips and tongue lazily caressed the pink nipples that soon were blossoming into hardness. "Quite clear," he repeated thickly.

In the long hours that followed, Jane wondered at one point if she could survive the physical and mental torment that seemed to be tearing her apart. Jake Dominic, the passionate lover who had brought her to the peak of ultimate ecstasy with skill and tenderness and then shuddered in her arms with his own fierce pleasure, was not this Jake Dominic.

This man also had incredible sexual expertise, but he used it with cool, calculated control. Time after time he used hands and lips that seemed to possess a devilish power to raise her to feverish need. There was no part of her body that was not caressed and probed and then caressed again, until she felt that there was not an inch of her flesh that was not exquisitely and painfully sensitized to his touch. He would toy with her like a large cat, his hot black eyes gleaming with savage satisfaction, until she was almost sobbing with frustrated desire. Then he would grant her completion in a burst of ruthless driving passion that would leave her shuddering like an exhausted and bruised swimmer cast upon the shore by a tidal wave.

Over and over the ritual of arousal and savage assuagement were repeated, until the silent tears were running down Jane's cheeks. Bewildered, she looked up at him as he crouched over her, his face a dark mask of brooding determination.

"Why?" she gasped desperately, her head moving back and forth on the pillow in an agony of response. "For God's sake, why, Jake?"

"Because you're mine," he said hoarsely as he drove forward between her thighs with explosive passion. "You may not be mine forever, but for now you belong to me." His words came out in a tormented rhythm caused by the force of his thrusting movements. "I won't have you smiling at, or touching, or even looking at, any other man. Do you understand?"

"Jake," she whimpered, striving desperately to marshal the words to explain, to entreat, but she was so lost in the heated haze of urgency that she could not speak.

"No one else, ever," he repeated relentlessly. "Do you understand?"

"Yes!" she almost screamed, digging her nails into his shoulders as the scarlet haze exploded into a thousand fiery tendrils of sensation.

It was almost dawn when Jake reached for her yet again, and suddenly her sobs no longer could be restrained. Jane found herself shaking and trembling in a reaction to the sensual assault that had no relation to love or affection.

Dominic froze, his body still for a long moment. Then, with a swift movement, he released her and reached out to flip on the bedside lamp. Turning once again to look at her, he started to curse violently as his eyes noted and comprehended his work.

Jane's eyes were dazed and shadowed with shock and misery, her lips swollen and bruised with the force of his lovemaking. She instinctively shrank away from him as his face darkened with a forbidding frown.

"God!" he said huskily, passing a trembling hand before his eyes, but not before she had seen the sick torment in their depths.

He reached out and plunged the room once more into darkness and pulled the sheet over both of them, tucking the cover carefully around her as if she were a small child. "Stop trembling," he growled, "I'm not going to touch you again."

He turned and lay on his back, his arms beneath his head. Even in the dimness of the darkened room Jane could see that his face was set and still as he stared sightlessly into the darkness. Her sobs were now reduced to mere ragged breaths. She was as bewildered by this reaction as she had been by his earlier savagery.

"I'll arrange to have Marc take you to the airport this morning," he said quietly.

She stared at him in alarm. Surely she hadn't made him this angry—not to the point of sending her away from him.

"Why?" she asked shakily, wiping her eyes on a corner of the sheet.

"Why!" he exclaimed bitterly. "My God, I've just used you as if you were a prostitute. I wanted to hurt you, and I set out to do it in the most humiliating and painful way possible." He laughed harshly. "My damned ego was damaged, so I decided that I'd prove that I could make you beg for it. And you ask me why?"

Jane tried desperately to think. Her mind was a muddle of emotions and half-formed ideas. There was only one clear thought shining through the morass. She must not be forced to leave Jake. This was perhaps the most significant and potentially dangerous moment in their relationship to date. If she couldn't relieve him of his guilt and bitterness, he might well send her away, and she could survive anything but that.

'It wasn't entirely your fault," she said tentatively. "I behaved badly at the nightclub."

"You're damn right you did," he said grimly, his voice hard. "If I hadn't known what was driving you, I would have strangled you. Instead, I took a revenge that I thought that I could enjoy."

He muttered a savage curse and fumbled in the drawer of the bedside table. Soon she heard the strike of a match, and the small flame briefly highlighted the planes of his face as he lit a cigarette. Then the flare was gone and there was only the orange-red tip of the cigarette glowing in the darkness.

"Did you think that I didn't know what was bothering you?" he asked bitterly. "I told you that you'd be running for the hills as soon as you got a taste of what living with me would be like." The tip of the cigarette flared bright as he inhaled deeply. "I admit that I didn't expect it to be after only one day."

"I'm not the one running away, Jake," Jane pointed out quietly. "You're the one who's rejecting me."

Jane could feel the sudden stillness of his body as he lay beside her. Then his voice came out of the darkness with savage deliberateness. "What are you, some kind of masochist? Do you like the idea of being abused? For God's sake, I can't even promise that it won't happen again." He turned to look at her, the glow of the cigarette casting a shadowy aureole over his features. His lips were twisted cynically, and his eyes held all the weariness of the world. "I'm a selfish bastard, and I have the devil's own temper. I've made it a habit to get whatever I've wanted for my entire adult life. It's not likely that I'll reform at this late date."

"I haven't asked you to reform," Jane whispered.

"I fell in love with the man you are, not some idealistic dream of what you could be."

"Very tolerant of you," he said mockingly. "I imagine you'd be less generous if I suddenly decided to savage you again."

A ghost of a smile curved her lips. "It would take a little getting used to, but who knows, I might get to like it," she said lightly. "Isn't forceful and repeated seduction by the man she loves supposed to be one of a woman's favorite fantasies?"

There was a blank silence, and then Jake chuckled. "You're really incredible, redhead." He shook his head in wonder. "Any minute now, you'll be thanking me for broadening your sexual experience and granting one of your fondest desires."

"I don't think I'd go that far," she said serenely. "But it's not as if I didn't enjoy some of it, Jake. It would have been physically impossible for me not to."

There was another long silence before Jake turned and crushed his cigarette in the ashtray on the table. He turned back to her and said abruptly, "I want to hold you." There was an oddly formal hesitancy in his voice. "Will you sleep in my arms, redhead?"

Jane felt an odd melting in the region of her heart. Would she ever understand this strange, complex man? Part devil, part little boy, and all tough, brilliant male.

"I'd like that," she answered softly.

She was immediately brought into the warm haven of his embrace, and her head nestled in the hollow of his shoulder. He held her as carefully and sexlessly as if she were a child.

"You won't send me away?" she asked sleepily, her body suddenly languid and exhausted in the warm security of his arms.

Jake kissed the top of her head. "No," he said thickly. "God, no!"

"Good," she said contentedly, rubbing her cheek like a kitten against the hard bone of his shoulder.

"Go to sleep, redhead." Jake spoke softly, his eyes alert in his dark face.

Jane relaxed obediently and was almost asleep when he spoke again, the words sounding oddly solemn and stiff, as if the sentiments were foreign to him, as indeed they were. "Jane," he whispered, his hand gently stroking her red curls, "I'm sorry."

She smiled drowsily and went peacefully to sleep.

Ten

When Jane opened her eyes, bright sunshine was streaming into the cabin and she was alone in the king-sized bed. A startled look at the digital clock on the bedside table told her why. It was almost one o'clock, and lunch was always served at one-thirty. Why hadn't Jake awakened her, for God's sake?

She jumped out of bed and headed for the shower, stopping only to pull a yellow terry-cloth robe from the closet. She stepped beneath the shower's steaming spray and closed the frosted cubicle door behind her. The pounding of the water on the tiles was so loud that she didn't hear Jake calling her name until he spoke right outside the shower stall. She immediately turned off the water and called back, "I didn't hear you, Jake. I'll be right out."

"No, stay where you are," Dominic said huskily. "I had to muster all my willpower to get out of bed and leave you, and I don't have much left. You walk out of that shower naked into my arms and it will all have been for nothing. I just came down to give you a message."

Jane's breath caught in her throat, and she could feel an electric jolt of desire at his words. There was something erotic about standing here naked and vulnerable and watching that virile shadow on the other side of the frosted door and knowing that he wanted her. "Message?" she asked, moistening her lips.

"Lola asked me to tell you that she'd like to say goodbye," Jake explained tersely. "She and Kahlid are taking the four o'clock plane to Las Vegas to do some gambling. She's in her cabin packing."

"Jake, you didn't—" Jane started to ask indignantly.

"No, I didn't suggest that they leave," Jake interrupted firmly. "Not that I wasn't planning on it, but Lola saved me the trouble. A very clever woman, our Lola."

After last night it was no more than Jane expected. "I'll go and see her as soon as I get out of the shower," she said softly.

"You do that." Jake's voice was oddly absent, and she could see the shadow move a step closer and his arm reach slowly for the handle of the door. Then the hand dropped and she heard a low curse and the shadow was suddenly gone.

It took her a moment to steady her breathing and the trembling of her hand before she could reach out and turn on the spray again. She let the soothing water pour over her and wash away all tension and soreness. Besides a slight stiffness and languidness, she felt no other signs of Jake's punishing lovemaking of last night. Her mind shied away instinctively from the thought of those savage passionate hours, but she firmly and deliberately focused her memory on the events both before and after.

She knew she must face and accept what had happened if she was to keep her love for Jake free from fear. She had been afraid for a little while last night, she admitted to herself. Yet she had known that Jake would never really hurt her physically, despite the cold anger that had prompted his actions. What had really frightened her was the terrifying sense of helplessness that she had experienced as she lay in his arms. He had manipulated her inexperienced body as if she were a puppet on a string, using his sexual expertise to dominate her until she'd felt as though she were being absorbed, her own spirit and personality melting away under the force of his greater experience.

She reached absently for the shampoo in the holder and began to shampoo her hair. It had really not been Jake's dominance she had feared, so much as her own inadequacy. Her hands paused in their scrubbing motion as the realization came home to her. Jane reviewed the evening with lightning swiftness. Yes, that was the underlying factor that had started all the tension and misery and almost caused Jake to send her away.

Even last night, when she had felt more glamorous than at any other time in her life, she'd been conscious of her pitiful inexperience in comparison to Jake's usual companions. She had felt miserably unsure when she had faced the sexy sophistication of blond Cindy Lockwood. Even Lola had been the focus of her subconscious envy.

Though Jake had seemed pleased with her responsiveness in bed and she couldn't help but be aware that he had derived an almost insatiable pleasure from their lovemaking, she was still beseiged with doubts. Was it only the novelty of their association that held him enthralled? Would he become bored once the newness of their relationship wore off? She had none of the tricks and skills of the experienced women who had graced his bed. The only advantage she might have over possible rivals was her boundless love.

So the problem was clear. In order to retain Jake's interest and her own confidence, she must become more knowledgeable. The pertinent question was, how she was going to get that expertise? She doubted that such knowledge could be obtained from books, though she was sure thousands had been written on the subject. She had no desire to experiment with any other man. Her forehead creased as she considered one possibility after another. Then her face cleared when the solution occurred to her. Of course—it was so simple. Why hadn't she thought of it before?

Jane hurriedly rinsed the shampoo from her hair and stepped out of the shower, drying herself swiftly and slipping on the yellow terry-cloth robe and matching scuffs. There wouldn't be time to dry her hair, she decided. She wrapped a towel turban fashion around her head and swiftly left the steaming bathroom.

In a matter of seconds she had crossed the short distance from the master suite to Lola Torres's cabin at the end of the corridor. She paused and drew a deep breath. Then, squaring her chin determinedly, she knocked firmly on the door.

Jake Dominic scowled darkly as he checked his wristwatch impatiently. Lola was already fifteen minutes late. Kahlid had finished saying his lengthy and cheerful farewells and was waiting in the launch with the seaman who was to take them to the pier at Cozumel. Lola's luggage had been collected and placed in the launch some thirty minutes ago, yet there was still no sign of her.

Then at last she came into view, and Jake relaxed fractionally as the Latin woman strode hurriedly toward him. An amused smile curved her lips when she saw the impatient frown on Dominic's face.

"Don't scowl at me, *querido*," she said lightly. "I would have been on time if it hadn't been for your *chère amie*. We have been having a little discussion."

"Why couldn't you have written her a letter?" Jake asked caustically. "Women have no sense of time!"

"You're such a chauvinist, Jake," Lola drawled. "Don't you know better than to resort to generalizations? I knew very well I was running late, but I felt that under the circumstances even you would rather I took the time to straighten out Jane's thinking."

Jake's eyes narrowed with sudden alertness. "And how did you accomplish that?" he asked slowly. "I was under the impression that Jane was a remarkably clear-thinking individual."

"In most areas I couldn't agree with you more," she said lightly, "But it seems the child has taken it into her head that she needs a tutor."

"Go on," Jake urged.

"Jane came to see me and asked my help," Lola reported, trying to keep a straight face, her eyes dancing. "It appears that she feels that she must improve her performance, and she elected to come to a professional."

"Performance?" Jake frowned, puzzled.

Lola's lips were quirking as she supplied a highly obscene Anglo Saxon noun.

"Oh, my God!" Jake groaned, and ran his hand through his hair.

Lola chuckled irrepressibly. "If only you could have seen her, Jake, sitting there like a prim and proper schoolgirl and trying to persuade me to give her lessons in the oldest profession in the world." Her dark eyes were gleaming with laughter. "All the while she was trying to phrase it with great delicacy, so as not to hurt my feelings! She was absolutely delicious."

"Very amusing," Jake said ironically, his expression far from amused. "I'm sure you were a great help to her."

"Oh, she had nothing so short term in mind," Lola said, her eyes twinkling. "She suggested that once you start your next picture, she'll join me in Los Angeles for some in-depth study. She seemed to think that, with work and concentration, it shouldn't take more than a few weeks."

"The hell she will!" Jake exploded, his face grim.

"I thought that would be your reaction," Lola said tranquilly. "I tried to explain that to our little friend."

"You take her up on that insanity and I'll take great pleasure in breaking that lovely neck of yours, Lola."

"Don't be absurd, Jake," Lola replied, affronted. "I like the child. I'm not about to get her into trouble with you," she added with a demure smile. "I even told her that you must be more than satisfied with her to reject my expert services. It's up to you to build up her confidence if you want her to forget this foolishness."

"Thanks for the advice," he remarked caustically. "I'll handle Jane in my own way, if you don't mind."

She shrugged. "I was only trying to help," she said, turning away to descend the ladder into the waiting launch. She turned back abruptly, her face serious. "The only reason I mentioned our conversation at all was that I don't think I convinced Jane. She seems remarkably single-minded."

"Remarkably," Dominic agreed dryly, his taut face echoing his exasperation. "I haven't the least doubt that she'll carry it through with all the subtlety of a steamroller. I'll have to watch her like a hawk or she'll be opportuning the madams of every bawdy house in L.A. for lessons."

Lola's dark eyes were gleaming. "There is another way, you know."

He looked at her inquiringly.

"You could tell her that you love her," she said.

Dominic's body stiffened as if she had struck him. His face was abruptly wiped free of expression, the dark eyes shuttered. "Could I?" he asked tonelessly. "It isn't usually your custom to meddle, Lola. I wouldn't advise you to start now." He gestured toward the waiting launch. "You have a plane to catch."

The music was as soft and sensuous as an intimate caress. They moved slowly around the dance floor, their arms wound around each other in the dimness of the crowded room. In the past few weeks Jane had noticed that in the wee hours of the morning the band at El Invernardero invariably discarded the lively disco numbers and played only mellow romantic tunes suited to lovers. This met with her complete approval, and she nestled closer to Jake with a sigh of contentment.

Jake looked down at her, his eyebrow cocked

inquiringly. "Tired?" he asked softly. "Would you like to go back to the yacht?"

She shook her head. "Not yet," she said dreamily. "I love to dance with you. Let's stay a little longer."

His arms tightened around her, but his voice was light. "Oh, for the energy of the young," he said, pulling a face. "Do you realize that this is the third time this week we've been here until four in the morning? You're going to make a physical wreck out of me, woman."

She looked up swiftly, her smile impudent. "You look in remarkably good shape to me in spite of our nights of dissipation," she said teasingly. "I didn't hear you complain when I suggested we come tonight."

Jake always looked devastatingly attractive in evening clothes, she thought. Tonight he was wearing the more conventional black tuxedo, and he looked as dangerous and virile as a stalking panther.

His eyes were flickering with mischief. "I wasn't anticipating a night on the tiles so much as my reward at the end of it," he murmured outrageously. "Gratitude always makes you more passionate."

They were both aware that this was patently untrue. He had only to touch her and Jane responded with all the combustibility of a brushfire in a windstorm. She looked back in wonderment on the casual, almost sexless woman she had been before Jake Dominic. He had thrown open all the doors of physical pleasure for her curious and delighted exploration, and she was as addicted to his lovemaking now as if it were the fruit of the poppy.

She suddenly grinned in amusement at the memory of the scene in Jake's cabin after Lola and Kahlid had left the *Sea Breeze*. He had been as outraged as a Victorian husband. While she had sat wide-eyed and cowed by his strong reaction to what had seemed to her a reasonable and simple solution to her problem, he had strode back and forth, wildly condemning her "harebrained" ideas with fluent and precise obscenities. He had then turned to face her with a forbidding frown.

"So help me God, I don't want to catch you so much as asking a question of *anyone*, other than the time of day! If you want to learn any little erotic variations, come to me, damn it. I believe I have sufficient experience to satisfy you!" He had stormed out of the cabin, slamming the door with explosive force behind him.

Jake's claim had proved a massive understatement, and she hadn't needed to ask. She found the variations mentioned no less exciting than the more conventional sex play, and she had embraced them with her usual enthusiasm. To her delight, Jake's passion for her had exhibited no signs of waning since Lola's departure, and in fact his hunger seemed to increase rather than diminish. At times he took her with an almost insatiable desperation that was as heady as strong wine and left her glowing with love and the faint stirrings of hope. He had never said he loved her even in the throes of the strongest passion, nor had he ever indicated that their relationship was anything more than temporary. But surely she must mean something to him if she could stir him to such heights of pleasure.

There were other moments, too, that promised much. Golden moments of shared laughter and more serious conversation, when the exploration of mind and emotion was as precious as that of their bodies. The man who spoke of his work with such single-minded passion was as far removed from the mocking playboy as night was from day. It was no wonder he was so successful at his craft, she had thought at one point, watching the eager flare in the usually jaded eyes. She felt a twinge of jealousy as she realized that here was a much more formidable rival than Cindy Lockwood or Lola Torres, and then dismissed the thought immediately as unworthy. She loved the total Jake Dominic, and the composite was created as much from the brilliance and drive of this other aspect of his personality as it was from the devilish charm and mercurial temperament that made her totally his.

Jane recognized that this was a halcyon period of jewel-bright days to be treasured and stored up against the time when she would no longer be Jake Dominic's sole interest. If she was to keep whatever affection he felt for her, she must release him to this other mistress. Her thoughts had been turning more and more frequently to that time when Jake would return to work, and she knew that she must be prepared to substitute another interest when it happened.

"You're very thoughtful, redhead," Dominic commented teasingly. "I think you're half asleep."

"I was wondering if I should begin thinking about a career," she said seriously.

The smile faded from Dominic's face as he pulled her possessively closer. "Plenty of time for that," he said impatiently. "It seems that I must redouble my efforts to keep you interested."

"No, really, Jake," she persisted. "Don't you think—"

"I think I want another glass of champagne," he interrupted abruptly, stopping in the middle of the dance floor. "And I think you're being much too serious." Keeping his arm firmly around her waist, he guided her swiftly among the dancers to their table.

As he pulled her chair out for her, he said lightly, "Did I tell you that you're completely captivating in that gown? You remind me of the cotton candy that I used to buy at the circus." He bent closer and bit gently on her left earlobe. "Pink, fluffy, and utterly delicious," he murmured.

The chiffon gown in question was a pink so pale it was almost white, and she knew it looked exceptionally good with her fiery curls. Since Jake had already commented on this curious phenomenon earlier in the evening, she recognized the compliment as an obvious ploy to distract her. She shot Jake an exasperated glance when he slipped into his own chair. She knew better than to try to pursue a subject when Jake wanted it dropped. He could be maddeningly elusive a times. She would just have to broach the subject when he was more amenable.

"I always thought of cotton candy as cloying, sticky-sweet stuff surrounding an empty cone," she said caustically, still annoyed with him.

He raised his glass to his lips, his black eyes amused. "No one could ever accuse you of being cloying and sticky-sweet, redhead," he said, his lips twitching. "And I assure you, I intend to make every effort to make sure that the cone is not empty tonight."

"Jake!" she said, color flooding her face. Would she never be able to control these damn blushes? she thought. Jake took a satanic delight in making these outrageous remarks just to see her light up like a Christmas tree. She looked across the table at his mocking devil's face and met his dark laughing eyes.

Suddenly Jake's face was no longer laughing, and his eyes were flickering with a different emotion entirely. Her breath caught as the world narrowed down to contain just the two of them, in the now-familiar pattern.

He put down his glass and said thickly, "It's time to go home, redhead."

She nodded dreamily and rose to her feet, gathering up her wispy pink wrap and the tiny brocade evening bag as he carelessly threw some bills on the table. She turned to precede him, and was startled by a sudden blinding light.

"Hold it, Mr. Dominic, just one more, please."

There was a muttered curse from behind her, and suddenly she was pushed aside. The plump, fortyish photographer in a gray business suit had time only to shout a frantic protest before Jake wrested the camera from him and dashed it to the floor with all his strength.

"My God, you've broken it!" the man yelped furiously. "That's an eight-hundred-dollar camera!"

"Send me the bill," Jake said icily. Grasping Jane

by the elbow, he pushed her through the whispering, staring crowd, his face white and strained with anger.

He was grimly silent on the taxi ride to the pier, his demeanor forbidding. It was only as the launch was nearing the *Sea Breeze* that Jane ventured to ask a question.

"Who was he?"

"Probably one of the freelance reporters who hang around resort towns and peddle their garbage to any rag that will print it," Dominic spat out.

"Was it wise to have gotten so violent?" she asked quietly. "Surely that will only make him more determined."

"Would you rather have your face spread over some scandal sheet as Jake Dominic's latest playmate?" he asked savagely.

"It wouldn't be pleasant," she admitted. "But it would be better than having you sued for damages."

"Forget it!" he ordered harshly. "I'll buy the bastard a new camera, and that will be the end of it."

Jane obediently subsided, but it was obvious that Jake did not forget the incident. He was moody and uncommunicative during the rest of the trip back to the yacht, and they had no sooner reached their cabin than he brought her forcefully into his arms.

There was a curious tinge of urgency in the way he stripped off the pink gown and tumbled her onto the bed. Tonight there were no preliminaries as he took her with a driving force that contained a bewildering element of desperation. There was an excitement all its own in his raw thrusting need, and when his strong body lay shuddering helplessly in her arms in an agony of release, she knew a satisfaction that was as primal as that of the first woman.

Eleven

The picture was really quite good of both of them, Jane thought absently as she spread the newspaper out on her lap. It was a Spanish-language newspaper, but the message would have been clear if it had been written in Swahili. Jake's possessive hand on her arm and the expression of dreamy desire on her own face told their own story. Lord, had she really been so transparent? She might just as well have worn a placard around her neck.

She looked up into Jake's face with wary eyes. It had been four days since the incident at El Invernardero, and Jake had been more moody and restless than she had ever seen him. Jane had been sunbathing in a deck chair when she had seen Jake striding toward her, his face a mask of rage, the newspaper clutched in his hand.

He had thrown the newspaper in her lap with a curt, "Look at this. That damn reporter sent it with the bill for his camera."

"He must have managed to salvage the film from the wreckage," she replied calmly. Her eyes ran swiftly over the accompanying story, and she breathed a sigh of relief. "It's mostly speculation and innuendo. I was afraid they might have stumbled on how I came to be on board the *Sea Breeze*." She made a wry face. "That would have been quite a scoop. Can't you see the headline: 'From bomb to bed!' "

"Jane!" Jake said savagely. "Don't you realize what this means? The A.P. is bound to pick up the story—it's too juicy to miss. In two days this picture will be in every newspaper in the world."

"I rather thought it would," Jane said quietly, folding the paper and dropping it distastefully to the deck. Her face was a little paler, but she smiled valiantly. "Well, it had to come sometime."

"Is that all you've got to say?" Jake asked hoarsely, his fists clenched in an effort to control the emotions that were running through him like high tide. He stooped to pick up the newspaper and waved it at her. "You'll be the topic of conversation and smutty little remarks over breakfast tables everywhere, and all you have to say is, 'It had to come sometime.' " He crumpled the newspaper into a ball and threw it over the rail into the sea.

"Aren't you overreacting?" she asked. "There have been dozens of other stories printed about you before with one woman or another and you obviously haven't given a damn."

Jake flinched, his face looking strangely vulnerable for a brief moment before it hardened into an unreadable mask. "Perhaps I'm getting tired of having my affairs publicized to give the masses a cheap thrill."

Jane gave him a skeptical glance. She knew that Jake couldn't care less what people thought of him. This violent reaction was completely out of character.

"It's not as if I hadn't known what to expect. I didn't walk into our relationship with my eyes closed. I knew that if I became your mistress, a certain amount of notoriety was inevitable. I accepted and came to terms with that fact a long time ago."

"How very adult and civilized of you," Jake snapped, his nostrils flaring. "Well, you're not going to have to test your sophistication in this instance. It's all over."

Jane sat bolt upright, shock and sudden panic

causing all color to ebb from her face. "I don't understand."

He turned and gazed unseeingly out at the sparkling sea, his hands tightly gripping the rail. His profile was frighteningly implacable. "I'm sending you home," he said ruthlessly. "I should have done it weeks ago."

"That's crazy," Jane protested dazedly, standing up and automatically slipping on her white beach coat. "Just because some little man takes our picture and manages to get it into a newspaper? It doesn't make sense."

"I'm finding the game not worth it," Jake replied harshly, still not looking at her. "You're just not worth the bother, Jane."

She felt as if he had driven his fist into her stomach, so blinding was the pain. "I don't believe you," she said numbly.

"Why not? You knew it had to end sometime. You've lasted longer than most."

She stepped closer and reached out to put a hand on his arm, instinctively trying to penetrate his hard facade by touch where words were proving useless. He flinched away from her as if she had burned him. "Don't touch me," he said through his teeth. "God, how I hate a woman who doesn't exit gracefully when shown the door." He turned to face her, his face granite-hard. "Do I have to say it? You're beginning to bore me. I don't want you."

Each word was like a whiplash on her raw emotions. Jane shook her head as if to clear it, feeling as though she were caught up in a nightmare. "It doesn't make sense," she repeated blankly. "Not like this. Not so suddenly."

He shrugged, his gaze once more on the horizon. "I want you on the plane this evening. You'd better pack."

As she stared at him, the certainty grew stronger that her instincts were correct. This reversal was entirely too abrupt to be genuine. He couldn't have made love to her with such wild passion only this morning and then decided that she bored him now.

"You're lying to me," she said huskily. "I don't know why you're acting this way; perhaps it's because of that photo in the paper. But I do know that you're not tired of me."

She could see his hands tighten on the rail until his knuckles whitened, but when he turned to look at her there was nothing but scorn in his dark eyes."My God, have you no pride? I've just told you that I don't want you anymore."

Her eyes were shining with tears as she wrapped her arms around herself to still the trembling that threatened to destroy her fragile control. "Yes, I have pride," she said simply. "If there ever comes a time when I believe that you don't want me, you won't have any trouble getting rid of me." She took a deep, shaky breath. "Until that time, not all the scorn and rejection in the world are going to keep me from fighting for you. You can force me to leave the *Sea Breeze*. You can even force me to get on that plane, but as soon as I get off the plane, I'll be on my way to the Coast. If you won't let me into your private life, I'll work and I'll study and I'll make myself so invaluable to you that you won't stand a chance of shutting me out of your work."

The tears were running freely down her cheeks now. "Damn you, Jake! Can't you see that what we've got is worth fighting for?"

For a moment there was a flicker of agony in the depths of Jake's eyes, and then he turned away. "I'll send someone down for your bags in an hour," he said without expression. "Be ready!"

"The hell I will!" For the first time Jane realized that it was really happening, that no amount of persuasion was going to shake that iron determination. She was going to be sent away.

She whirled and walked blindly from him, so lost in a haze of pain and misery that she cannoned into Marc Benjamin. With a broken apology, her face a strained mask of agony, she pushed past him, stumbling dazedly in the direction of their cabin.

Benjamin gave a soundless whistle as he gazed after the vulnerable little figure, before he turned back and approached Jake Dominic with a grim smile on his face. He waved the folded newspaper in his hand. "I guess I don't have to ask if you saw this little item," he said, tossing the paper casually on the deck chair. "I see Jane is pretty upset by it all."

Jake turned to face him, and Benjamin inhaled sharply. Jake's face wore the expression of a man suffering the tortures of hell. The dark eyes, which usually mirrored only mockery and cynicism, were wells of pain and torment.

"Have the launch prepared, Marc," Jake said dully, "and arrange to have someone go down and pick up her luggage in about an hour. Jane will be taking the evening plane to Miami."

Benjamin's face reflected his surprise. "I never thought she'd be that upset by this trash," he said thoughtfully, gesturing contemptuously at the newspaper on the deck chair. "I'd have bet it would have taken considerably more than that to make her leave you."

Jake's mirthless laugh was like the snarl of an animal in pain. "Oh, God, yes," he said bitterly. "If I'd let her, the little fool would have stayed and let the world smear her with the same filth that they attribute to me." His fist struck the rail. "Damn it, she even said she expected it!"

"She's a sensible girl in spite of all that idealism," Benjamin said slowly. "Jane always knew what she'd be facing, but she didn't care."

"Well, I care, damn it!" Jake said passionately. "I'm not going to stand by and let them hurt her. God, do you realize what a year as my mistress could do to a girl like Jane?"

"She wouldn't change," Benjamin said confidently. "The girl is stronger than you think." He looked at Jake's face speculatively, and the torment he saw there prompted him to make a suggestion. "Of course, there's another way that you could protect her if you chose. You could marry her."

Jake looked at him scornfully. "Do you think that I haven't thought of that?" he asked bitterly. "Don't you think that I'd like to reach out and grab what I want, just as I have all my life?" He shook his head, his lips thinned in a line of pain. "My God, I'm seventeen years older than Jane and a hundred years older in experience. Even a dissipated bastard like me knows that she deserves better than that." He smiled bitterly. "I've done her enough damage by making her my mistress." His hand struck the rail again. "But damn it, I wanted something for myself!"

"You love her," Benjamin stated, with wonder coloring his voice.

"Of course I love her," he said impatiently. "Who the hell wouldn't?" His eyes narrowed to brooding darkness. "She's like a vase of the finest crystal, absolutely clear, with none of the distortions and impurities that plague most of the rest of us."

Benjamin's lips quirked. Dominic was not only completely crazy about Jane, he was waxing lyrical. "I can't see the problem," he said. "Lord knows, the girl is mad enough about you."

"She'll get over it," Jake said harshly. "You know as well as I do that she needs someone as fresh and wholesome as herself for a lasting relationship."

"I'm not at all sure of that," Benjamin said slowly, "I rather think that Jane might need someone older and more experienced to take care of her."

There was a brief flash of hope in Jake's face before he shook his head. "Thanks for trying, Marc," he said morosely, "but I know that I'm right about this. She'll be better off without me."

"I'm not giving you some bull to give you an excuse for doing what you want to do," Benjamin said bluntly, his voice rough with impatience. "For God's sake, shake off that martyr's air and look at the girl's record to date. She's gotten herself mixed up with a bunch of crackpots and almost blown up the

Sea Breeze. She nearly got herself raped or killed at that cockfight in San Miguel. She came within an inch of being devoured by a shark. To top it all off, she's become the mistress of one of the most notorious men in the Western world. Now, this has all taken place in the space of less than two months. Heaven knows what other trouble she's gotten herself into that I'm not aware of." He smiled grimly. "Personally, I don't know any wholesome young man on the face of the earth who could have handled all of that!"

There was a stunned expression on Jake's face. "You're absolutely right, you don't have the complete list," he breathed softly. "God, Jane's a walking time bomb!"

Coolly Benjamin regarded the dawning uncertainty on Jake's face. "You should also consider that a girl like Jane isn't going to recover from any love affair very easily. She's not the type to bounce back and locate this paragon you've mentally linked her with any time soon. It's far more likely that she would look around for some kind of work to take her mind off you." Benjamin's eyes narrowed thoughtfully. "Yes, she'll probably revert to her original plan."

Jake looked up swiftly, alarmed. "What original plan?" he demanded.

"The Peace Corps," Benjamin answered blandly.

"The Peace Corps?" Dominic echoed blankly.

Benjamin nodded. "She confided to Simon that she'd been considering joining for some time. She seemed to think that they'd take her like a shot. She'd be a godsend to them, with all the languages she knows."

Jake's dark eyes were dazed. "Jane in the Peace Corps!"

Benjamin smiled gently. "It's more than likely they would assign her to the Middle East. Kahlid was very impressed with her command of Arabic, wasn't he?"

Burying his face in his hands, Jake groaned. "Good

Lord, even the United States Government couldn't make that big a mistake!"

"They'd snap her up, and you know it," Benjamin said bluntly. "Young, intelligent, charismatic, *and* fluent in several languages."

"No!" Dominic almost shouted, his hands dropping from his face as he whirled to confront Benjamin. His dark eyes were wild and blazing. "In six months' time she'd be in a Middle East bordello or decorating the post outside some head hunter's hut." He ran his hand through his crisp dark hair. "Do you think that I'm going to spend the rest of my life worried about what kind of trouble she's going to get herself into next? No, by God!" He turned and strode furiously away, every line of his tall muscular body breathing fiery determination.

Benjamin gazed after him with a curiously enigmatic smile on his face before turning and strolling back to the bridge.

Jane was still in the peach bikini and the white terry beach coat when Dominic stalked into the cabin. She looked up from throwing things haphazardly into an overnight case on the bed, her cheeks wet with tears. "My hour isn't up yet, but I'm almost finished packing," she said defiantly. She closed and snapped the lock on the suitcase. "This is all I'm taking. You can give all the rest of those Diors and St. Laurents and whatevers to someone else."

"I suppose camouflage denims and khaki jungle shorts would be more practical for what you have in mind," he spat out, glaring at her furiously. "Well, you can just forget about it. Do you hear me? I'm not going to stand for it!"

She looked at him, puzzlement mixed with indignation in her golden eyes. It wasn't enough that the man was destroying her life, rejecting her, tearing her emotions to shreds. Now he had the gall to march in here and shout at her!

"I have no idea what you're talking about," she

said belligerently. "I wish you'd just get out of here so that I can finish dressing. I wouldn't want to be late for that plane you're so anxious for me to catch."

"To hell with the plane!" he muttered. "You're coming with me, damn it!" He grabbed her by the wrist and pulled her, struggling and protesting from the cabin. He strode purposefully down the corridor and up on the deck.

"Jake, let me go!" Jane gasped furiously. "I'm tired of being carried and pulled and pushed around like some sort of glorified piece of luggage. Will you please treat me with a little dignity?"

"Be quiet," Jake said between his teeth, pushing her ahead of him into the lounge. "You're insane if you think I'm going to let you make my life hell on earth. You can just forget about that bloody Peace Corps. You're going to marry me, damn it!"

Jane shook her head dazedly. Peace Corps? Then his last statement sank in.

"Marry you?" she whispered, her eyes widening so that they were enormous in her pale face.

"Marc has full authority to marry us on the high seas," Dominic said, striding toward the phone at the bar and dragging her along behind him. "I'm giving orders for us to get underway. In thirty minutes we'll be out of Mexican territorial waters." He reached for the phone, but she suddenly put her hand on the receiver and stopped him.

"Why, Jake?" Jane asked quietly, her face pale and tense. "Why do you want to marry me?"

"Why do you think?" he replied bitterly. "Because I'm a selfish bastard who can't even do one decent, unselfish thing to insure your well-being. I don't give a tinker's damn anymore if I'll be good for you or not. I'm grabbing you and holding on, come hell or high water."

Jane felt hope flower in her, its golden petals tentatively opening to a beautiful, unbelievable possibility. "But why?" she persisted, her eyes shining like jewels in her heart-shaped face.

"Because I love you!" he snapped, his face grim.

"Because I don't care what's right or wrong, or even what's best for you, as long as I can keep you with me for the rest of our lives."

Jane closed her eyes and took a deep breath. It seemed too gloriously, wonderfully perfect to be real. When she opened her eyes, Jake caught his breath at the glowing, starlike radiance in their depths.

She moved forward slowly, her arms slipping around his waist and her cheek nestling against his chest with a touching childishness, "You're not joking?" she asked huskily. "You really love me?"

Jake's arms went around her, and his voice was suspiciously ragged when he said, "I love you, redhead." One hand left her waist to press her head closer to his heart. "And may God help you, because I can't let you go." His hand tangled in the silky curls and tilted back her head to look down into her glowing face. His features were curiously vulnerable, and the dark eyes held an uncertainty that was foreign to them. "Last chance, sweetheart," he said thickly. "Tell me no now, and I might be able to muster enough willpower to stop myself. Once you're committed, I'll be the only man in your bed and in your life for the rest of your days."

"I told you once that I'd never say no to you," Jane replied firmly. "That hasn't changed, and it never will."

Dominic lowered his head and covered her lips in a kiss that was as solemn and binding as an exchange of wedding bands. When their lips parted, they were both shaking and clinging to each other like two lost children.

"You don't have to marry me, you know," Jane whispered. "All I ever wanted was for you to love me. I can understand if you'd rather not be tied down."

Jake kissed her lightly on the tip of her nose. "You may not mind living in sin, you shameless woman, but I find my reactions are verging on the primitive and the puritanical where you're concerned," he said, only half joking. "I want to tie you to me with every bond I can lay my hands on." His crooked eyebrow arched mockingly. "I hope you're not having second thoughts, because I've shed my last scruples. You're mine now—forever."

"You don't think that you may regret it later?" Jane persisted, a worried frown on her face. "I don't think I could stand it if it didn't last."

Jake's face was unusually solemn as he said, "You're my first love, my last love, and my only love, Jane. I didn't even think the emotion existed, until you walked into my life and turned it upside down. I'll never be able to do without you now."

He released her hair and reached over her head to pick up the phone receiver. Holding her close with one arm, he gave the order to get underway.

After he hung up the receiver, he slid his other arm around her and lowered his head to kiss her with a honeyed sweetness. Pushing aside the beach coat, his hand slid inside to caress the bare satin flesh of her waist and back. Then suddenly his lips were no longer sweet but hot and hungry, parting her lips with his tongue to probe and explore with suffocating passion. Jane instinctively arched to meet his body's arousal, and his hand wandered down to cup her rounded buttocks in his palm and bring her up against his thrusting loins.

Suddenly she pressed both hands against his chest and pushed, wriggling out of his arms at the same time. "No," she gasped breathlessly, her face flushed and her golden eyes clouded with passion. "I want to talk."

Surprise at her sudden rejection was mirrored in Jake's eyes, and his face reflected the temptation to ignore her verbal plea and attend only to the message that was still emanating from her aroused body. Then his own body relaxed slightly, though his eyes were glazed and hungry as they fixed on her full, swollen breasts in the tiny peach bikini.

"There's distinct evidence that you have ambivalent emotions on that score," he teased. "But I'll let you get away with it for now, redhead. Talk!"

Jane closed the beach coat hurriedly and backed away from him, her cheeks pink. She walked over to the brown leather couch in the center of the room and sat down. Tucking her feet under her, she looked over the back of it at Jake, still standing by the bar. She patted the seat beside her invitingly, and he obediently strolled over and dropped down beside her.

His dark eyes were dancing with mischief as he said softly, "Now you really know that I love you, sweetheart. I've never stopped at a moment like that in my entire life."

"How long have you loved me?" she asked eagerly, folding her hands before her on her lap. An expression of warm tenderness lit up Jake's cynical face; it would have astounded those who thought they knew him.

"Forever," he said simply.

"No, really, Jake," she demanded.

"I suppose that I knew for sure that night in San Miguel when I ran out the door and saw you buried under that pile of men," he said, grinning. "I didn't know whether to beat you or pick you up and run away with you. I'd never felt like that before, and it scared the hell out of me." He reached out to rub a finger along the sensitive curve of her lower lip. "Before that I was aware that you affected me more than any person I'd ever met—man, woman, or child—but I wouldn't admit that it was anything more than liking and a strange sense of protectiveness."

"Why didn't you tell me?" Jane asked indignantly. "I told you the very day that I found out."

Jake shook his head, his mouth twisting. "For the first time in my life I decided to be noble. I knew damn well I didn't have any right to you. I'm seventeen years older and have forgotten more wickedness and deviltry than you could ever imagine. I knew I should have sent you away the minute I realized what had happened to me, but I convinced myself that I could keep you near me and at least have these two months for myself."

His fingers slid down to rest in the hollow of her

throat, stroking the sensitive pulse point sensuously. "Then everything blew up in my face. Between that damn shark and Kahlid, my good intentions flew out the window. I couldn't keep my hands off you. I rationalized my taking you to bed by telling myself that the only way to discourage you was to show you that it was a losing proposition." His lips tightened grimly. "That was a bunch of bull. I was wild for you. I wanted you more than I'd ever wanted anything in my life, and I reached out and took what I wanted."

Jane smiled with gentle irony. "It's no wonder you felt guilty. Anyone could see how unwilling I was."

Dominic's eyes became even warmer as he said, "God, you're sweet. I can't get enough of you." He shook his head ruefully. "I'd never had anyone respond to me with such open passion and affection. You had me as dizzy as a schoolboy."

His fingers moved from the hollow of her throat to slip under the beach coat and clasp one bare shoulder. He bent to lay his lips on the soft hollow that his fingers had just abandoned. Jane could feel her pulse leap as his tongue gently, leisurely probed the silky hollow.

"Yet you would have sent me away," she charged breathlessly, her hand moving irresistibly to caress the crispness of his thick dark hair.

"I'm a masochist," he said mockingly as his lips moved to nibble enticingly at her earlobe. "I knew it would kill me, but I couldn't stand seeing you smeared over every yellow-journalism sheet in the world. I'd taken enough from you without that."

"Thank God you overcame your scruples," Jane said huskily. "I had visions of having to pursue you on every film set in Hollywood."

He gave her ear a sharp nip that was far from loverlike. "And I had visions of having to rescue you from everything from white slavers to man-eating lions. I don't want to hear anything more about this passion for the Peace Corps."

Jane wondered dreamily what on earth he was

talking about, but as his other hand reached under the beach coat to lightly cup one eager young breast, she promptly lost track of the conversation. What had he said? Oh, yes, something about the Peace Corps. "They do very good work," she said vaguely, while Jake's hands located the catch of the bikini top and released it.

"So do I," he said mischievously, and proceeded to prove his claim with deft erotic hands and tongue. "And I'm never letting you venture any farther from me than the next room," he said hoarsely after several wild, heated moments.

Suddenly he was rising and crossing the lounge with swift steps. He shot the lock on the door, and as he turned back to her, he was already starting to unbutton his cream shirt. He unbuttoned the rest while he walked slowly back to the couch. She stared at him with yearning and fascination as he stripped off the shirt and threw it on the chair.

There was a teasing smile on Jake's face despite the leaping flame in his dark eyes. He gently pushed the beach coat off Jane's shoulders, and let it drop in a white pool on the brown leather couch.

"It just occurred to me that we're missing a once-in-a-lifetime opportunity," he said thickly as his thumbs stroked her nipples teasingly. "In another hour, we'll be just another old, stodgy married couple. This is our last chance to taste the forbidden fruits of living in sin. I don't think we can afford to pass it up, do you?"

Her arms slid around his neck and slowly pulled him down into her eager embrace. "It would be quite a shocking waste," she agreed happily. "I think you're absolutely right."

"You're damn right I am, redhead," Jake said with mocking arrogance, and bore her back on the couch.

Fabulous News for Iris Johansen Fans!

From the spellbinding pen of this multi-talented author comes her most lush, dramatic, and emotionally touching romances yet—three magnificent love stories about characters whose lives have been touched by a legendary statue, the Wind Dancer.

ON SALE NEXT MONTH . . .

THE WIND DANCER

IRIS JOHANSEN has romance reviewers and noted romance writers raving about the advance copy they read of this thrilling historical romance!

A glorious antiquity, the Wind Dancer is a statue of a Pegasus that is encrusted with jewels . . . but whose worth is beyond the value of its precious stones, gold, and artistry. The Wind Dancer's origins are shrouded in the mists of time . . . and only a chosen few can leash its mysterious powers.

A magnificent love story, WIND DANCER is set in Renaissance Italy where intrigues were as intricate as carved cathedral doors and affairs of state were ruled by affairs of the bedchamber. This is the captivating tale of the lovely and indomitable slave Sanchia and the man who bought her on a back street in Florence. Passionate, powerful Lionello Andreas would love Sanchia and endanger her with equal wild abandon as he sought to win back the prize possession of his family, the Wind Dancer.

The Wind Dancer was born of a white-hot bolt of
     lightning.
So legend has it.

The Wind Dancer's worth was beyond price; its beauty
     beyond belief.
So legend has it.

The Wind Dancer could punish the evil, could reward
     the good.
So legend has it.

The Wind Dancer wielded the power to alter the
     destinies of men and nations.
So legend has it.

But legend, like history, can be distorted by time,
     robbed of truth by cynicism—
   yet be gifted with splendor by imagination.

In the following brief excerpt you'll see why *Romantic Times* said about Iris Johansen and THE WIND DANCER: "The formidable talent of Iris Johansen blazes into incandescent brilliance in this highly original, mesmerizing love story."

We join the story as the evil Caprino, who runs a ring of prostitutes and thieves in Florence, is forcing young heroine Sanchia to "audition" as a thief for the great *condottiere* Lionello who waits in the piazza with his friend Lorenzo, observing from a short distance.

"You're late." Caprino jerked Sanchia into the shadows of the arcade surrounding the piazza.

■ ══════════════ ■

"It couldn't be helped," Sanchia said breathlessly. "There was an accident . . . and we didn't get finished until the hour tolled . . . and then I had to wait until Giovanni left to take the—"

Caprino silenced the flow of words with an impatient motion of his hand. "There he is." He nodded across the crowded piazza. "The big man in the wine-colored velvet cape listening to the storyteller."

Sanchia's gaze followed Caprino's to the man standing in front of the platform. He was more than big, he was a giant, she thought gloomily. The careless arrogance in the man's stance bespoke perfect confidence in his ability to deal with any circumstances and, if he caught her, he'd probably use his big strong hands to crush her head like a walnut. Well, she was too tired to worry about that now. It had been over thirty hours since she had slept. Perhaps it was just as well she was almost too exhausted to care what happened to her. Fear must not make her as clumsy as she had been yesterday. She was at least glad the giant appeared able to afford to lose a few ducats. The richness of his clothing indicated he must either be a great lord or a prosperous merchant.

"Go." Caprino gave her a little push out onto the piazza. "Now."

She pulled her shawl over her head to shadow her face and hurried toward the platform where a man was telling a story, accompanying himself on the lyre. A drop of rain struck her face; and she glanced up at the suddenly dark skies. Not yet, she thought with exasperation. If it started to rain in earnest the people crowding the piazza would run for shelter and she would have to follow the velvet-clad giant until he put himself into a situation that allowed her to make the snatch.

Another drop splashed her hand, and her anxious gaze flew to the giant. His attention was still fixed on the storyteller, but only the saints knew how long he would remain engrossed. This storyteller was not very good. Her pace quickened as she flowed like a shadow into the crowd surrounding the platform.

Garlic, Lion thought, as the odor assaulted his nostrils. Garlic, spoiled fish, and some other stench that smelled even fouler. He glanced around the crowd trying to identify the source of the smell. The people surrounding the platform were the same ones he had studied moments before, trying to search out Caprino's thief. The only new arrival was a thin woman dressed in a shabby gray gown, an equally ragged woolen shawl covering her head. She moved away from the edge of the crowd and started to hurry across the piazza. The stench faded with her departure and Lion drew a deep breath. *Dio*, luck was with him in this, at least. He was not at all pleased at being forced to stand in the rain waiting for Caprino to produce his master thief.

"It's done," Lorenzo muttered, suddenly at Lion's side. He had been watching from the far side of the crowd. Now he said more loudly, "As sweet a snatch as I've ever seen."

"What?" Frowning, Lion gazed at him. "There was no—" He broke off as he glanced down at his belt. The pouch was gone; only the severed cords remained in his belt. "Sweet Jesus." His gaze flew around the piazza. "Who?"

"The lovely madonna who looked like a beggar maid and smelled like a decaying corpse." Lorenzo nodded toward the arched arcade. "She disappeared behind that column, and I'll wager you'll find Caprino lurking there with her, counting your ducats."

Lion started toward the column. "A woman," he murmured. "I didn't expect a woman. How good is she?"

Lorenzo fell into step with him. "Very good."

Lion leaned back in his chair. His gaze went again to the smooth flesh of her shoulders. "And I like the shade of your skin. It reminds me of the gold of—" He stopped. He had been going to compare her to the Wind Dancer, he realized with a sense of shock. It must have been Lorenzo's remark that had brought the connection to mind. Possession. The Wind Dancer. Sanchia.

He lifted his goblet to his lips. "You know why you're here?"

"Yes." She moistened her lips with her tongue. "I knew when I saw you looking at me when I was in the bath. It's the same way Giovanni looked at my mother. You want to use my body."

The comparison irritated him. "I'm not Ballano," Lion said harshly.

"You had me bathed. You had me perfumed." She drew a quivering breath. "Do you want me to take off this gown and kneel on the floor now?"

"No!" The explosive rejection surprised him as much as it did her. "There are more pleasurable ways of taking a woman than if she were a bitch in heat."

"Yet the idea excited you," Sanchia said. "I saw that you were—"

"You see too much." A sudden thought struck him. "Are you trying to change my mind by comparing me to Ballano? Lorenzo said you use every weapon you possess."

"But I have no weapons here," she said simply. "I gave you my promise that I'd obey you."

No weapons. Lorenzo had said that, too, Lion recalled with frustration. She belonged to him. It was his right to use her body as he chose, with either tenderness or brutality. She knew this and accepted it. Why, then, was he feeling as if he had to make excuses for bedding her? "It doesn't have to be as it was with Ballano. I'll give you pleasure and—"

"No." Her eyes widened with bewilderment. "Why do you lie to me? It's always the man who has the pleasure. Women are merely vessels who accept them into their bodies and take their seed. Never once did my mother have pleasure."

"Because she was treated like an animal." Lion set the goblet down on the windowsill with a force that splashed the remaining wine on the polished wood. "I'll show you ways . . ." He stopped as he saw she was looking at him with complete disbelief.

He smiled with sudden recklessness. "Ah, a challenge. Shall I make you a promise, my doubting Sanchia? Suppose I tell you that I'll not use you as my 'vessel' until you beg me to do it. Until you're willing to kneel and let me use you as Giovanni did your mother because you yearn to have me inside you."

She looked at him in wonder. "Why should you make me a promise? You need not consider my feelings. I belong to you. It doesn't matter if I feel nothing when—"

"It matters to me." His tone held exasperation as well as barely concealed violence. "God knows why, but it does." He took her hand and pulled her to her knees before his chair. "And I'll probably regret that promise a thousand times before this is over. Now lift your head and look at me."

She obediently tilted back her head and she caught her breath at what she saw in his face. His eyes held dark, exotic mysteries and the curve of his lips was blatantly sensual.

"What do you see?"

"You want me."

"Yes." His big hands fell heavily on her slender shoulders. "And whenever I look at you from now on I'll be thinking of what I'd like to do to you." One callused hand released her shoulder and began to stroke her throat. Her skin was as velvet-soft as it lookea dn warm, so warm. . . . He felt hot lust tear through him, adding dimension to his manhood. "I'm going to touch you whenever I like." He slipped the material of the gown off her shoulders. "When it pleases me, I'll bare this pretty flesh and fondle you. No matter where we are. No matter who is watching."

She was gazing at him if mesmerized, the pulse fluttering wildly in the hollow of her throat.

"Are you a virgin?"

She moistened her lips with her tongue. "Yes."

"Good." He felt a primitive jolt of satisfaction so deep it almost obliterated the memory of Lorenzo's words.

■ ═══════════════════ ■

Just to whet your appetite even more, read what two of your favorite romance authors have to say about

THE WIND DANCER.

"IRIS JOHANSEN IS A BESTSELLING AUTHOR FOR THE BEST OF REASONS — SHE'S A WONDERFUL STORYTELLER. SANCHIA, LION, LORENZO, AND CATERINA WILL WRAP THEMSELVES AROUND YOUR HEART AND MOVE RIGHT IN. ENJOY, I DID!"

—Catherine Coulter,
New York Times bestselling
author of *Secret Song*

"SO COMPELLING, SO UNFORGETTABLE A PAGE TURNER, THIS ENTHRALLING TALE COULD HAVE BEEN WRITTEN ONLY BY IRIS JOHANSEN. I NEVER WANTED TO LEAVE THE WORLD SHE CREATED WITH SANCHIA AND LION AT ITS CENTER."

—Julie Garwood,
New York Times bestselling
author of *Guardian Angel*

ASK YOUR BOOKSELLER TO RESERVE A COPY OF THE WIND DANCER FOR YOU. IT GOES ON SALE IN THE BEGINNING OF JANUARY . . . AND READING IT IS THE ONLY WAY TO START OFF YOUR NEW YEAR!

The next engrossing book by Iris Johansen about those whose lives are enmeshed with the fate of the Wind Dancer is—

STORM WINDS

ON SALE IN MAY 1991

A glorious romance, STORM WINDS is set against all the turbulence and promise of the French Revolution. Clever and daring banker Jean Marc must retrieve the Wind Dancer from Marie Antoinette for his ill and aging father. Jean Marc's schemes lead him from the danger of Paris, to the tranquil gardens of southern France, to the perilous mountains of Spain. But soon his passion for the quest is overshadowed by his growing love for the one woman who can fulfill his dreams, the fiery artist Juliette.

A Must Read Romance!

And the breathlessly exciting climax to the books featuring that fabulous statue of the Wind Dancer is—

REAP THE WIND

ON SALE IN OCTOBER 1991

This is the riveting, fast-paced, utterly dazzling contemporary love story of passion and revenge that sweeps from exotic eastern bazaars to elegant perfumeries of Paris. Cynical and brilliant Alex Karzov pursues the Wind Dancer to use as an instrument of revenge. Caitlin, a woman as exquisite as the perfumes she creates, is at first only a means to an end for Alex . . . until he falls desperately in love with her and realizes he has endangered her more than he has his mortal enemy.

A MAGNIFICENT TRILOGY . . .

ALL FEATURING THE MYSTERIOUSLY POWERFUL STATUE, THE WIND DANCER

ALL TO BE PUBLISHED IN 1991

DON'T MISS THE BIGGEST LOVE AFFAIR IN PUBLISHING IN 1991

THE LATEST IN BOOKS AND AUDIO CASSETTES

Paperbacks

☐	28671	**NOBODY'S FAULT** Nancy Holmes	$5.95
☐	28412	**A SEASON OF SWANS** Celeste De Blasis	$5.95
☐	28354	**SEDUCTION** Amanda Quick	$4.50
☐	28594	**SURRENDER** Amanda Quick	$4.50
☐	28435	**WORLD OF DIFFERENCE** Leonia Blair	$5.95
☐	28416	**RIGHTFULLY MINE** Doris Mortman	$5.95
☐	27032	**FIRST BORN** Doris Mortman	$4.95
☐	27283	**BRAZEN VIRTUE** Nora Roberts	$4.50
☐	27891	**PEOPLE LIKE US** Dominick Dunne	$4.95
☐	27260	**WILD SWAN** Celeste De Blasis	$5.95
☐	25692	**SWAN'S CHANCE** Celeste De Blasis	$5.95
☐	27790	**A WOMAN OF SUBSTANCE** Barbara Taylor Bradford	$5.95

Audio

☐ **SEPTEMBER** by Rosamunde Pilcher
Performance by Lynn Redgrave
180 Mins. Double Cassette   45241-X $15.95

☐ **THE SHELL SEEKERS** by Rosamunde Pilcher
Performance by Lynn Redgrave
180 Mins. Double Cassette   48183-9 $14.95

☐ **COLD SASSY TREE** by Olive Ann Burns
Performance by Richard Thomas
180 Mins. Double Cassette   45166-9 $14.95

☐ **NOBODY'S FAULT** by Nancy Holmes
Performance by Geraldine James
180 Mins. Double Cassette   45250-9 $14.95

Bantam Books, Dept. FBS, 414 East Golf Road, Des Plaines, IL 60016

Please send me the items I have checked above. I am enclosing $_____
(please add $2.50 to cover postage and handling). Send check or money order,
no cash or C.O.D.s please. (Tape offer good in USA only.)

Mr/Ms _____

Address _____

City/State _____ Zip _____

Please allow four to six weeks for delivery.   FBS–1/91
Prices and availability subject to change without notice.

60 Minutes to a Better, More Beautiful You!

Now it's easier than ever to awaken your sensuality, stay slim forever—even make yourself irresistible. With Bantam's bestselling subliminal audio tapes, you're only 60 minutes away from a better, more beautiful you!

__ 45004-2	**Slim Forever**	$8.95
__ 45112-X	**Awaken Your Sensuality**	$7.95
__ 45035-2	**Stop Smoking Forever**	$8.95
__ 45130-8	**Develop Your Intuition**	$7.95
__ 45022-0	**Positively Change Your Life**	$8.95
__ 45154-5	**Get What You Want**	$7.95
__ 45041-7	**Stress Free Forever**	$8.95
__ 45106-5	**Get a Good Night's Sleep**	$7.95
__ 45094-8	**Improve Your Concentration**	$7.95
__ 45172-3	**Develop A Perfect Memory**	$8.95

Bantam Books, Dept. LT, 414 East Golf Road, Des Plaines, IL 60016

Please send me the items I have checked above. I am enclosing $_____ (please add $2.00 to cover postage and handling). Send check or money order, no cash or C.O.D.s please. (Tape offer good in USA only.)

Mr/Ms _____

Address _____

City/State _____ Zip_____

LT-5/90

Please allow four to six weeks for delivery.
Prices and availability subject to change without notice.